Do a Dare, Earn a Charm, Change Your Life

I picked up my dad's P-Com, his hand-sized portable computer for e-mail and appointments . . . I thoughtfully added a few pop-up reminders to help him out in his busy life.

September 4: Take Carmen shopping for school clothes.

September 10: Dinner with Carmen at Mondo Taco.

September 12: Carmen needs new shoes.

September 15—

The screen went blank.
Then it came back on.

Make up a cheer using the words dive, goat, and processed cheese.

Blue and white fireworks exploded around the message.

Then the screen went blank.

Not only did I have a psycho cheerleader for a stepsister, it looked like my dad's electronics were going psycho, too.

Carmen Dives In

Linda Johns

MIRROR
STONE

Carmen Dives In
©2005 Wizards of the Coast, Inc.

All characters in this book are fictitious. Any resemblance to actual persons, living or dead, is purely coincidental.

This book is protected under the copyright laws of the United States of America. Any reproduction or unauthorized use of the material or artwork contained herein is prohibited without the express written permission of Wizards of the Coast, Inc.

Distributed in the United States by Holtzbrinck Publishing. Distributed in Canada by Fenn Ltd.

Distributed to the hobby, toy, and comic trade in the United States and Canada by regional distributors.

Distributed worldwide by Wizards of the Coast, Inc. and regional distributors.

Star Sisterz, Wizards of the Coast, Mirrorstone and their respective logos are trademarks of Wizards of the Coast, Inc., in the U.S.A. and other countries.

All Wizards of the Coast characters, character names, and the distinctive likenesses thereof are property of Wizards of the Coast, Inc.

Printed in the U.S.A.

The sale of this book without its cover has not been authorized by the publisher. If you purchased this book without a cover, you should be aware that neither the author nor the publisher has received payment for this "stripped book."

Cover art by Taia Morley
Interior art by Yasuyo Dunnett
First Printing: April 2005
Library of Congress Catalog Card Number: 2004116890

9 8 7 6 5 4 3 2 1

US ISBN: 0-7869-3714-9
ISBN-13: 978-0-7869-3714-1
620-17763-001-EN

U.S., CANADA,   EUROPEAN HEADQUARTERS
ASIA, PACIFIC, & LATIN AMERICA   Wizards of the Coast, Belgium
Wizards of the Coast, Inc.   T Hofveld 6d
P.O. Box 707   1702 Groot-Bijgaarden
Renton, WA 98057-0707   Belgium
+1-800-324-6496   +322 457 3350

Visit our website at www.mirrorstonebooks.com

To Star Sisterz Rachel Guyer-Mafune
and Sarah Sliker and my star
of a sister Nancy Heard

Chapter 1

The Mobile Blogger
Friday, September 3

If you want to know the meaning of "My Life Sucks," just ask your ordinary ninth grade girl at Middletown High. In fact, you could ask me. I fit that description—

I put my head down on the keyboard. "This is pathetic."

"What's pathetic?" My stepbrother, Sam, poked his head in the door of my dad's office.

Oops. I hadn't realized I was talking out loud.

"Um, nothing," I mumbled, trying to cover up my laptop screen. "I'm . . . I'm just working on some assignment."

"Assignment? For what? School hasn't even started

yet." Sam was talking to me, but looking at his skateboard. He's a total boardhead. He worships that thing.

"Not really an assignment," I said. "Just something optional to do before LA-9A." (That's the abbreviation for Language Arts 9, as in ninth grade, and A, as in first semester.)

"You know what's pathetic?" Sam said. "Your school, that's what. It sounds totally lame." Sam and his skateboard left.

Didn't Sam realize that if my school was totally lame, his school was, too? Besides, it isn't school that's pathetic. It's my life that's pathetic.

You see, my dad is remarried to this woman named Michelle Benson, who has two kids and—you guessed it—Sam is one of them. So now, after fourteen years of being an only child and the hands-down favorite, I suddenly had a brother.

Not a cute little kindergarten kind of brother. Not an older brother with a driver's license and cool friends named Ethan and Luke.

No.

What I have is a brother MY SAME AGE.

Yes, folks, that's right. When the bell rang to start the school year on Tuesday morning, Step-Sam and I would both be ninth graders at Middletown High.

It was an entirely awful situation.

Now that I have your sympathy, you're probably wondering if anything can possibly be worse.

Well, yes. It can.

Because Step-Sam came with an older sister. Riley's a junior who is gorgeous and popular and perfect in just about every way imaginable.

That is why I felt compelled to hate her.

Things were bad enough when Dad and Michelle got married last year. But then at the beginning of the summer they announced that they were moving into Middletown to be closer to the lab where Michelle works. Dad said it was also to be closer to me. He said he wanted "all three of my kids" to go to the same high school.

Blech! Suddenly Riley and Sam were his kids? I'd spent fourteen years perfecting the art of being an only child, and I didn't appreciate those two imposters suddenly horning in on my father.

My dad, David Bernstein, is a political reporter for *The Middletown Free Press.* Maybe you've heard of him? He always has stories on the front page.

All summer, Dad worried about Riley and Sam going to a new school.

Hello? Dad? It's a new school for me, too! The leap from Middletown Middle (such an unfortunate name) to Middletown High is a big deal. But my dad didn't seem to notice.

He thought it would be a good idea if I spent Labor Day weekend with him so Riley and Sam could bond with me before school started. He promised to take time off work so he could spend the whole weekend with us. But at the last minute, a big story broke, and he got called in to cover it.

So now here I was on Labor Day weekend, the last weekend of the summer, alone with the Steps.

Normally, I would have escaped to one of my friend's houses. But no one was around. Most normal families in Middletown go away for a last summer hurrah before school starts. My best friend Brooklyn was jumping off the dock into Badger Lake, paddling around on an air mattress, and eating ice cream bars. My other best friend Rachel was lying out on the beach. Meanwhile, I couldn't even go swimming at the Aqua Dive pool, since it was closed for the holiday weekend.

At least, I had my dog, Murphy, with me. I patted Murphy's head and settled back in Dad's office chair.

Okay. Enough of me feeling sorry for myself (although there is obviously plenty of material here for me to have a weekend-long Pity Party).

Time to get back to my blog.

I glanced at the screen. "D'oh!" I moaned out loud. Murphy raised his head and looked at me.

The screen was blank. I'd deleted everything I'd written.

"Truly pathetic," I mumbled to myself as I shut down my laptop. The Mobile Blogger would have to wait.

Oh yeah, there's one other thing you should know about me. I'm a blogger. A secret blogger, actually. I write a web log that offers a look at the life of a brilliant and witty American teenage girl (that would be me) now entering her freshman year of high school. I write about real stuff. Like books and movies. Friendships. Feelings. Sure, sometimes I write about clothes and shoes. But only in the larger social context. (Such as, what to wear on the first day of high school to appear confident yet not too eager to impress.)

If Riley, my stepsister, were a blogger, her blog would be all about fashion, boys, who's popular and who's not. But Riley isn't a blogger. At least, I don't think she is.

Of course, she doesn't know that I'm a blogger. No one knows. That's right. None of the approximately thirty-two people who have visited The Mobile Blogger have any idea who writes it. Thirty-two readers might not sound like a lot. But just last month it was only eighteen. At this rate, I'll have a thousand by the time I graduate from college.

From the kitchen, I heard Riley squealing.

"Oh, honey, that's so great! I'm so proud of you!" I could hear my stepmom Michelle gushing.

"I know!" Riley said. "I'm so excited! I have to go tell Carmen."

I opened up the laptop again to look busy.

"Carmen! Guess what!" Riley bounced into Dad's office with a smile so bright and white it would make the model from a toothpaste commercial jealous. She was holding these ridiculous pom-poms with blue and white streamers.

"Um, blue is your new favorite color?" I guessed.

Apparently, Riley didn't catch my sarcastic tone.

"Oh, I always liked blue," Riley said, shaking the streamers above her head and twirling around on tiptoes. "But now I love it! And I'll be wearing a lot more of it now that I'm a varsity cheerleader for the Middletown Sharks!"

"But you don't even go to school there yet," I said.

"I know. That's what's so great!" she said, coming to a sudden stop in her spin.

I wondered if she was crazy. Maybe she was some kind of psycho cheerleader wannabe and she'd show up at school in a cheerleading outfit and try to cheer at games, even though she wasn't on the squad. Now that's an interesting thought: My perfect and popular stepsister is really a psycho cheerleader. This kind of made-for-TV-movie story might get more readers to my blog.

"Um, Riley?" I was using a gentle voice, which sounded like the one the psychiatrist uses on *Law and Justice* when trying to get the facts from a deranged suspect. "You haven't started school yet, and you didn't try out for the squad, but suddenly you're a cheerleader at Middletown?"

Riley looked at me like *I* was the crazy one. "Apparently, the cheer advisor, Ms. McDermott?"

I thought she wanted me to nod, so I did. I had never heard of a Ms. McDermott at Middletown High. But good for Riley for making up a believable name on the spot. I wanted to encourage my psycho stepsister to keep going with her story, so I nodded again enthusiastically.

"Yeah, so Ms. McDermott is friends with Ms. Whitney, my old advisor at West Valley High. Ms. McDermott told Ms. Whitney about how the Middletown cheer squad didn't have any veterans, because they were all seniors last year. Ms. McDermott said they could use someone like me, with experience. She saw my work last year at West Valley."

Her work? As if cheerleading was some kind of art. Oh, man. This was delicious. The move to a new high school had seriously thrown Riley off the deep end. I couldn't wait to tell Brooklyn about the weekend's top news story: Former West Valley cheerleader goes psycho.

Riley was still gushing. "So Ms. Whitney told Ms. McDermott I was going to Middletown High this year. And Ms. McDermott got all excited and worked it all out!"

Suddenly Michelle appeared and gave Riley a big hug. "Isn't it great?"

I nodded mutely. I haven't exactly warmed up to Michelle the Stepmom yet, and now I wondered about her judgment. She was clearly encouraging her daughter's potentially unstable—not to mention embarrassing—behavior.

"I was so worried about you, honey, not getting to cheer this year. I know how much you put into it, and it was just going to be such a big void in your life." Michelle nuzzled her prized offspring. "I'm so happy everything worked out! And you look so good in blue!"

Riley threw up the pom-poms and spun around again, ending her spin with a hug for her mom. Clearly Riley agreed that she looked good in blue. I plastered a big smile on my face. I felt as phony as a, well, as a cheerleader.

"So, Riley, did one of the old cheerleaders quit or something?" I asked, still fake-smiling.

Riley shrugged. "No. They just added me to the squad. So what are the other cheerleaders like?"

"I don't know. I haven't actually gone to Middletown High yet, remember? I'm just a freshman. It's a new school for me, too."

"Oh, right," Riley said, sounding disappointed. "I keep forgetting. So that means you don't even know who the cheerleaders are?"

I nodded. Wow. Way to make me feel like a loser. I hadn't until that moment realized my lack of association with the MHS cheerleaders left such a hole in my life.

Riley quickly recovered her smile. "In that case, we'll both have so many new people to meet!"

Riley headed for the door. Her walk looked even bouncier than usual. "Mom and I have to go to Mall-O-Rama and get a few things before practice this afternoon. That's when Ms. McDermott is going to officially introduce me to the rest of the squad. I'll give you the full 4-1-1 at dinner tonight."

"Carmen, would you like to come with us?" Michelle asked.

"No, thanks," I said, pretending to be looking at something on my computer screen. "I'm just waiting for my dad to get home." I put a big emphasis on the word *my*.

Michelle flinched a bit. I felt bad. But I wanted to make sure that Michelle and Riley remembered that David Bernstein is *my* dad. I've known him a lot longer than either of them.

A few minutes later, the front door closed and I heard the car pull out of the driveway.

Finally, I was alone again.

I picked up my dad's P-Com, his hand-sized portable computer for e-mail and appointments.

I scrolled through his calendar. It looked like he had to go to a three o'clock press conference today. Since *The Free Press* is a morning newspaper, that would mean Dad would be back at the paper filing his story and wouldn't be home until about eight o'clock or so. Darn.

I scrolled through the rest of his calendar, and I thoughtfully added a few pop-up reminders to help him out in his busy life.

September 4: Take Carmen shopping for school clothes.

September 10: Dinner with Carmen at Mondo Taco.

September 12: Carmen needs new shoes.

September 15—

The screen went blank.
Then it came back on.

Make up a cheer using the words dive, goat, and processed cheese.

"Huh?" I said out loud.

The screen flashed again.

I said: Make up a cheer using the words dive, goat, and processed cheese.

Blue and white fireworks exploded around the message.

Then the screen went blank.

Not only did I have a psycho cheerleader for a stepsister, it looked like my dad's electronics were going psycho, too.

A chilling thought took over my brain. All joking aside, what if Riley was really nutso? What if she was so obsessed with being a cheerleader that it was her sole mission in life, and she was leaving her rah-rah touch on everything—including my dad's stuff?

I should be concerned with Riley's mental health, right? But all I could think about was myself.

I had a boardhead dork for a stepbrother, and a deranged cheerleader for a stepsister. How perfectly pathetic.

And what a rotten way to start high school.

Chapter 2

Soon enough, it was Tuesday morning, and my first day at Middletown High. Mom gave me a ride to school.

"Don't get used to this," she said. "This is only a first day of school thing."

"Got it," I said. "But with all the pressures facing me today, I think it might have been a form of teen abuse if you'd made me ride the bus."

"You could have ridden your bike, you know," Mom said. "It saves gas and prevents air pollution."

"Riding a bike is so last year," I said in my best Mall-O-Rama Girl voice.

Mom took a quick glance at me. I tried not to smile. Because everyone knows I absolutely love to ride my bike. Earlier in the summer, Mom and I had gone on a three-day eighty-mile bike ride with the Valley Cycling

Club. Sometimes she rode her bike to work. She was always talking about not wasting gas. She even drove a hybrid car. They're supposed to be good for the environment or something. While I'm all for preserving the environment, the truth is I like to ride my orange 24-speed road bike because it's just plain fun. But not on the first day of school. No way.

We pulled into the parking lot.

"Oh, look! There's Riley and Sam," Mom said with a bit of forced enthusiasm. "What great timing."

The Steps were driving up in this huge boat of a car. I am not kidding. This thing looked like it could hold a dozen people for a three-day cruise. It had only two doors, but it was about as long as the super-jumbo van that I used to take to Camp Connemara. And the thing was old. I'm no judge of cars, but this is the kind of car my grandpa might have driven even before my mom was born.

"Would you look at that?" Mom said. "A '64 Plymouth."

A blast of blue smoke blew out the back right before Riley turned off the engine.

"I'm looking. Did you see that smoke? Talk about pollution. Gross!"

Mom must not have been listening to me. "They don't make them like that anymore," she said wistfully.

"Nope. They sure don't make them like that any more . . . because no one would buy them."

My voice didn't seem to be registering with Mom.

"Riley! I love your car!" Mom rolled down her window and called out to my stepsister, as she stepped out of her giant boat-car. "My uncle had a '64 just like that."

I couldn't believe my ears. I was expecting Mom to make a comment about the big gas-guzzling pollution machine, not provide a positive review.

"Hi Carmen! Hi Bridget!" Riley shut her door and bounced over happily to Mom's window, with Sam trailing behind her. "This was my dad's car when he was in high school. He just gave it to Sam and me last night."

"Hey, Riley!" Two girls, with perfect blond hair and bright white smiles came rushing over.

"Cheerleader alert," I heard Sam mumble. He was already walking away.

How is it you can tell who's a cheerleader even without the little outfit and the pompoms? It must be the non-stop smiles and the perky walk.

"Great practice yesterday, Riley," the taller girl said.

"Thanks, Madison," Riley said. "I just hope I'm ready for Friday's game."

"Oh, you will be!" the two girls chimed. They hooked arms with Riley, and she was off in an immediate rush of popularity. This confirmed it. Riley was a popular cheerleader, not a psycho cheerleader. Still there was a slight chance that she was the one who put that weird processed cheese message in Dad's P-Com. I'd have to keep an eye on her.

I said good-bye to Mom and watched her pull off in her non-gas-guzzling, hybrid car.

"Carmen!" My two best friends in the entire world, Brooklyn and Rachel, called to me from the front steps.

"Nice jeans," Brooklyn said, when I caught up to them. Brooklyn bent down and tugged at my freshly shrunk and perfectly unassuming jeans.

Brooklyn's been the tallest of the three of us ever since third grade. She could be a model with her thick, wavy black hair and dark olive skin.

Rachel flipped her long brown glamour girl hair. "Yeah, those jeans will be nice and cool when it gets to be 95 degrees at noon."

We all giggled. We'd obsessed the night before about what to wear on the first day of high school. It was important to not look like we cared too much. But we had to care a little. So, like all good Middletown girls, we'd been at Mall-O-Rama in August getting some new clothes. I'd decided at ten o'clock last night, after about a thousand phone calls, that I'd wear jeans, flip-flops, and a new snug T-shirt that said "The Who." Very retro.

We all pulled out our schedules and compared them for about the thirtieth time. Not only did I have my own schedule memorized, I had both of theirs committed to memory too. Unfortunately, Brooklyn and I didn't have a class together until third period. Brooklyn and Rachel started off in Spanish together, but I was on my own for the first one hour and fifty minutes of my high school career.

"At least we have third together," Brooklyn said. "Since that's homeroom, it's fifteen minutes longer."

"I, on the other hand, will be stranded with who knows what mutants for the longest period of the day," Rachel said, as the first-period bell rang. "I'll see you guys at lunch."

Finally. Third period. LA 9A. In just about every ninth-grade Language Arts class across the country, students would be reading *Great Expectations* by Charles Dickens this quarter. At least that's what Ms. Neimo said as she gave her speech: "What to Expect Now That You're in High School."

More than half the class now had great expectations to hate the book.

"But I'm getting ahead of myself," Ms. Neimo said. "First, I'll take roll and we'll go over some of our home-room announcements."

What is it about taking attendance that makes me nervous? All I have to do is wait for my name to be called and raise my hand and say, "Here." But as soon as a teacher starts, I sit up a little straighter and feel my heart beating a little faster. And I get nervous right away, seeing as how my last name, Bernstein, starts with a "B" and there aren't usually that many people ahead of me in alphabetical order.

"Margie Alfonso," Ms. Neimo read.

"Here."

"Todd Arrington. Eric Barnes."

Two more "here's."

"Sam Benson."

Oh yeah. I forgot to tell you. Step-Sam is in my Language Arts class. The horror!

"Carmen? Carmen Bernstein?"

I snapped back to attention. "Here?" I said, with a slight wave of my hand.

Ms. Neimo smiled at me. But some kids snickered.

"She said your name three times," Brooklyn whispered to me, as Ms. Neimo continued calling roll.

My face flushed red.

"Brooklyn Cicero?"

"Here!" Brooklyn chimed in clearly and immediately went back to whispering to me. Apparently she doesn't get that same roll-call nervousness that I do.

"So, what was Sam Benson like over the weekend?" Brooklyn asked.

"Step-Sam? I hardly saw him. Didn't see Riley much, either. I can NOT tell you how happy I was when Murphy and I got back to our house."

"Okay, people" Ms. Neimo said. "I'm not a big fan of alphabetical order. But in this case, I don't have a choice. I'm going to assign your locker partners in alphabetical order. And no, you cannot trade. This order was determined by the office, so if you have any issues, you'll need to take it up with someone down there."

Alphabetical order? Locker partners? I could feel my face heating up again. Benson, Bernstein. Was I doomed to keep getting trapped with Step-Sam?

"Let's see, Sam, you'll be with . . ." Ms. Neimo started, looking at her list.

Please don't say my name. Please don't say my name. Please don't say my name.

". . . Car . . . " Ms. Neimo was pausing.

Not Carmen. Not Carmen. Not Carmen.

". . . Carpenter. Aidan Carpenter and Sam Benson, come up and get your locker number and combination. Then go out and try it a few times. Next we'll have Carmen Bernstein and Brooklyn Cicero."

Whew! Ms. Neimo handed Brooklyn a notecard that said *392* at the top. When we got out to the hall, we high-fived. Totally uncool, I know. But this meant we'd be locker partners for the entire year.

I had been such a ditz, worrying about having to share a locker with Sam. I mean, it's bad enough I have to share my dad with him. But a locker? What was I thinking? Guys share with guys. Girls share with girls. I was such a total freak I hadn't been thinking straight. All that anxiety for nothing.

Locker number 392 was full-length and had a fresh coat of pea soup green paint. I don't understand why, when new paint is involved, schools don't choose some better colors. But MHS seemed committed to a barf-inspired color scheme. Oh well. Soon Brooklyn and I could decorate the inside and claim it as our own. That is, if we could ever get it open.

"Here, let me try," I said, nudging Brooklyn over. "Read the combination to me."

"I can't read it out loud. What if someone hears it?" Brooklyn said in an exaggerated—and loud—whisper.

"Since I'll never be able to memorize ours," Nova said. "I think your secret is safe."

I don't know Nova that well. We have a different circle of friends. But I've always thought she was cool, ever since third grade when she was especially nice to me during four-square. She's a library person, like me. You know, the kind of people who choose to go to the library over the summer. Anyway, she and Samantha had the locker right next to ours.

"This must be why they made third period extra long," Brooklyn said. "I hope it doesn't take fifteen minutes every time we try to open this thing."

"Got it!" I said, triumphantly opening up Locker 392, after only forty-two tries. Brooklyn and I each did it two more times, just to make sure we had the hang of it. Then we headed back into class.

"Okay, we have a little more business to take care of," Ms. Neimo said.

Everyone quieted down.

"We have many, many opportunities for you to get involved as freshmen at Middletown High." It seemed like she had reams and reams of flyers to hand out to us. "If you have any questions about any of the teams or clubs, I can try to answer them. And if I don't know, I'll get an answer for you by tomorrow," she said, above the din of paper passing.

An aquamarine flyer caught my eye: *Dive in to MHS Swim Team!*

Brooklyn held hers up.

"Perfect for you!" she mouthed.

I didn't say anything.

On one hand, Brooklyn was right. When I was in elementary school, my family got a membership to the

Aqua Dive, and I would swim there for hours. A true water baby, my parents said. (I was born February 7, so I'm an Aquarius. The water sign.)

My mom kept trying to get me to join the swim team, but there was one problem. You see, to be on swim team, you have to dive. And that was one thing I would not do. I was afraid to dive. Not just afraid. Terrified. Horrified. Scared stiff. Paralyzed with fear. Diving, to me, was the stuff of nightmares.

For a brief, crazed moment, I actually considered trying out anyway. But then, a few desks over, I heard Todd talking to Sam.

"Dive in! Dude! That's perfect for you!" Todd turned to Eric and pointed to Sam. "This dude won first place in six swim meets at the city pool this summer."

Eric gave Sam a high-five. "Great! You've got to get a spot on our team."

Sam was grinning from ear to ear, looking down at the swim team flyer.

I folded mine in half and stuck it in my notebook.

"Now there are just a couple of spots left open on the staff of the *Weekly Shark*," Ms. Neimo handed out a tabloid-sized newspaper. "Here's the first issue of the year, prepared by some students who came in last week to get things going. We'll have room for a couple of freshmen. The first meeting is after school tomorrow."

She seemed to be looking at me.

And why not? My dad, David Bernstein, is a great reporter. And I am the (secret) Mobile Blogger. It's like writing is in our Bernstein blood. I can be an investigative journalist, star reporter, and diva with a dazzling pen.

Who needs swim team?

The Mobile Blogger
Tuesday, September 7

First day at Middletown High. What are you wearing? Come on, admit it. You thought about it for at least a week in advance. Maybe you even got some new threads at the Mall-O-Rama. Maybe you even wore a new black turtleneck, just so you'd look cool, despite the fact that it was about 105 degrees inside Mr. Stredwick's math class. Maybe you bought new jeans. And then you washed them three dozen times in the last week, trying to make them look not so obviously new. (Wait until the parental units get the water bill. Ouch!)

How long did it take you to get your locker combo to work? The worst part was going back to the locker after lunch, and then trying to unlock it. I felt like there was a big clock ticking over my head, counting down the seconds until I'd be late for fourth period. All because I can't remember "right 32, left 18 . . ." Wait! I can't tell you my locker combination.

I can't say I made any new friends or that the earth shook for me when Ms. Neimo said we'd be reading *Great Expectations*. Hung out with friends from Middletown Middle. Felt intimidated by the juniors and seniors. Secretly watched boys. And tried the Pita Special in the cafeteria. FYI, it does not live up to its sign's claims: "Pita Special . . . because it's pretty special."

I wonder what Wednesday's lunch special will be? That is the biggest thing on my mind as I begin my high school journey. Ha!

Chapter 3

At 3:10 p.m. on the second day of school, I, Carmen Bernstein, began my journalism career.

I mention my last name here because my dad, also a Bernstein and also a journalist, idolized this famous reporter named Carl Bernstein.

This Bernstein guy did a huge story that exposed a scandal with President Richard Nixon. Ever heard of Watergate? That's the story. Being a famous reporter is hardly as impressive as being a rock star, but my dad thought Carl Bernstein was a hero.

Get it? Carl Bernstein? Carmen Bernstein?

Cute, huh? Yeah, I didn't think so.

I was mulling all this over and anticipating my own big stories as I headed back up to Room 304, Ms. Neimo's room, and the official office of the Middletown High *Weekly Shark*.

There were about ten people scattered around the room. One girl looked up at me and sort of smiled. At least I hoped it was a smile. I didn't know anyone in the room, so I just sat down and started reading the newest issue of the paper.

At 3:15 p.m., a guy in jeans, black-and-white checked sneakers, and a skateboard shirt stood up.

"Okay, we might as well get started," he said. "I'm Elliott Goodman."

"We know that," said a girl with purple-fringed hair and a pierced nose. She'd definitely perfected the bored tone.

"You know that, Sloan, but I see a couple of new faces here," Elliott said, staring at me and this girl with long curly brown hair. She was in my LA-9A class, and I think her name was Sarah something. We must have been the only newbies.

Elliott cleared his throat. "Let's go around and introduce ourselves. I already said my name. I'm the editor in chief." He had the obvious confidence of an upperclassman. "This is my fourth year at the *Shark*," he added. That would make him a senior.

"I'm Sloan Kettridge," the purple-fringed girl said. "I'm the music and movie reviewer."

Of course.

It was my turn.

"Um, I'm Carmen Bernstein. I'm a freshman."

Sloan rolled her eyes. "Hey, freshman, could you pass me that plate of crackers and that processed cheese?"

Huh? Who says "processed cheese"? Wasn't that one of the weird, lame words in that secret message on my dad's P-Com? I did a double-take at Sloan. I was sure I'd never seen her before. You'd think I'd remember.

I reached to the desk next to me and grabbed a plate of crackers and cheese, and handed it over to her.

"Hmmmm . . . processed cheese," Anthony, the guy next to Sloan, said in a Homer Simpson voice.

What was going on? Was there some kind of processed cheese fad sweeping the streets of Middletown? I put all cheesy thoughts out of my head and tried to focus on the meeting.

Elliott handed out the production schedule with the upcoming deadlines for the next month. Turns out that the *Weekly Shark* isn't really a weekly after all. It's a biweekly, published every other week.

I raised my hand tentatively.

"You don't need to raise your hand, Karen, just speak out like a real reporter at a press conference," Elliott said.

"It's Carmen," I said. "My name is Carmen. And I'm just wondering why you call it the *Weekly Shark* when it isn't really a weekly."

Sloan snorted and Anthony laughed.

"Well, Carmen, we thought the name 'Bi-Weekly Shark' made us too easy of a target for some of our esteemed colleagues here on campus. So we call it a weekly and wait to see if the brilliant minds of Middletown High will be smart enough to catch on. So far, no one's commented."

Everyone laughed. It was clear that the Shark staff thought they were all pretty dang smart. And that everyone else was a lame brain.

"Ms. Neimo is going to work with you two freshmen on your first assignments," Elliott said. "Think of this as your tryout article."

I was not going to let myself be intimidated by Elliott, purple-haired Sloan, Anthony, or the other upperclassmen. I was going to write the best story the Shark has ever had. I couldn't wait to see my assignment.

"These are the official assignment sheets you'll get for each story," Ms. Neimo explained, holding two pieces of paper in her hand. "The sheet tells the subject of your story, how many words you need to write, and your deadline. Under 'comments' you'll sometimes find suggested names of people to interview or other resources to use. Here's yours, Carmen."

I couldn't believe it.

My mind started spinning. Maybe I could write a riveting exposé on why in the world they let someone (a.k.a. Riley) on the squad when she didn't even try out. I could instantly become a big name on campus with this scoop.

Then the spinning from my brain moved down to my stomach. Did I have the guts to carry off an article that might hurt someone's feelings? Not just any someone, but my own stepsister?

For forty-five glorious minutes that night, I felt completely free. Mom and I go to the Aqua Dive for adult lap swim at least four or five times a week. Once we get into our swimsuits, we don't talk. We have this understanding that pool time is private time.

We headed from the shower to the deck in silence. I was still adjusting my goggles when Mom dived in and started her laps. I slipped into the shallow end gracefully. At least that's how I like to imagine it in my head. The truth was that I looked more like I was stumbling into the pool.

Mom swam over to me. "Someday, you're just going to dive in, Carmen. I just know it," she said. She smiled and I almost believed her. Then she was off doing the breaststroke.

Dive! There was another one of those awful words kicking around in my head. Dive, goat, and processed cheese. I started swimming my warm-up lap. I could perfectly see the way Dad's screen looked when that message flashed at me. *Make up a cheer using the words dive, goat, and processed cheese.*

If someone started talking about goats, I'd know there was some sort of global conspiracy to make me whacko. I'm not sure what the point of the conspiracy would be, but it would obviously be directed at me. Maybe the entire world was a laboratory and I was the experiment.

My every move was being documented. Some social scientist posed a question: "What would a fourteen-year-old girl do when given a secret nonsense message?"

And then the crazed researchers were off testing me.

The Mobile Blogger
Wednesday, September 8

Have you ever thought about processed cheese? What is that stuff? One time, back when I didn't mind being seen in public with my parental units, we all went to Miller's Food Stop to stock up on salty snacks for a Super Bowl party. My dad sent me off to get some Watson's CheeseStuff. He said he had this killer recipe for a nacho-dip, and it would only work if he used two jars of Watson's. So while Dad headed for the chip aisle, I headed to the big blue letters that said DAIRY. Man! I had no idea there were so many kinds of cheese. Gouda, Swiss, havarti, muenster, brie, parmesan, bleu, jack, feta. There was even a big display of California cheese. (Since when was California known for its cheese?)

But no Watson's.

I went back to tell Dad the bad news. Like, maybe they'd stopped making his favorite cheese back in the

1970s or something. I mean, there's probably not a lot of demand for the stuff.

Dad refused to give up. He went and found a clerk, who immediately pointed him to Aisle 8A. The "Snack" aisle.

Have you ever been to the end of Aisle 8A at Miller's? Let me tell you, it's a trip. Because that's where you'll find an entire shelf of Watson's Cheese-Stuff varieties of soft-processed American cheese. It comes in jars. It comes sliced. It comes in tubes. It comes in cans so you can spritz your CheeseStuff into fancy little shapes on your crackers. You could spell out your name with your Watson's CheeseStuff EZ-Squeeze Tube. Spread it. Slice it. Melt it. According to WatsonCheeseStuff.com, the possibilities are unlimited.

But here's the freaky part: The stuff isn't refrigerated.

Remember in seventh-grade science with Ms. Casalas when we learned about bacteria, and we even grew some of our own on our desks? Using old bits of cheese? Wouldn't you expect that Watson's unrefrigerated bright orange cheese would be a breeding ground for bacteria? Well, apparently it's not. All those delicious chemicals keep Watson's bacteria-free.

Well, enough of this cheesy tale. Or should I say processed cheesy tale? You don't see the stuff around Middletown High much. Not many of us have jars of Watson's in our lunch boxes. (But you could keep a jar in your locker for snack breaks. I'm telling you, the stuff lasts for forty years.) Anyway, I got a whiff of some processed cheese after school today. Actually, I didn't get a whiff. Because the stuff doesn't really smell. But I did admire its lovely orange hue.

Comments

If you enjoy processed cheese, perhaps you should try some cheese-flavored snacks as well. I'll bring some in my lunch. We can trade.

    P.S. Who are you?

posted by T-Bone, September 8, 9:23 P.M.

Do I know you? Because we had some processed cheese at the *Shark* today. Watson's, in fact.

posted by WriterGrrl, September 8, 9:23 P.M.

Chapter 4

Hey, Riley." I hesitated as I approached my step-sister the next day at school. We're supposed to be sisters and all, but let's face it. Riley is a junior. She goes on dates. With BOYS. She can drive. And she's a cheerleader.

"Carmen! Hi!" Riley gushed. "I'm so happy to see you! How are things going?" She linked arms with me. We started walking out of the Middletown High lobby and down the hallway. "Where are you going? Can we walk and talk? Do you want to go to lunch today? Oh, wait. I forgot. Freshmen can't go off campus." She paused for half a beat, then went on. "But that's okay. I can stay on campus and have lunch with you, if you want!"

"Actually, I have a favor to ask you," I began. I felt so nervous. I wonder if Katie Couric from NBC News ever feels like a total dweeb when asking for an interview.

"A favor? You bet! What is it? Do you want to borrow clothes? Because I have a new periwinkle sweater that would look so killer on you! And I bet it would fit. You might be a little smaller in the chest than me, but it would still look great." Riley looked at me expectantly, and then she went on. She was kind of like that non-stop bunny that's powered by batteries. "Or maybe if you don't like periwinkle, you could try my lavender one. I haven't worn it here yet, so no one would know. It would be so fab with your coloring!"

"Thanks, Riley, but I don't need to borrow clothes," I said.

"You don't?"

She had a tone in her voice that said, *Are you crazy? Of course you need to borrow my super cute clothes and get rid of your total loser Middletown Middle School leftover wardrobe.*

"No, but thanks. Really. The thing is, Riley, I'm doing a story for the *Weekly Shark* on the cheerleaders . . ."

"Ohhhhh!" Riley squealed before I could finish my sentence. "What an absolutely fabulous idea for a story! Did you think of it? Because that's a great way to get noticed! Write about something that everybody loves, and then everybody will love you. It's a sure-fire way to get popular!"

"Actually, it was assigned to me."

Riley looked disappointed.

"But I jumped at the chance, of course. Because I knew what a great story this could be. Especially since they added a cheerleader to the squad. People will want to know all about you and where you came from."

"Yes, I bet they will," Riley said wistfully. "I bet everyone is super curious about me."

"So, the thing is, I'd like to come to a couple of practices, to see how hard you all work and the kinds of things you have to do." I was totally playing up to her.

"That's a great idea!" Riley said. "You can come today, after school. We have a ninety-minute practice on Thursdays. I can introduce you to all the girls. They're all so great. I just love them. I feel like they're the sisters I never had."

I looked at Riley.

"I mean, you're my stepsister and all, but I hardly know you. And these girls just have so much in common with me. We all love to dance. Our favorite band is Suburban Voice. We all love periwinkle blue. It's like we're the same person!"

I had to stop myself from saying anything snotty.

"Thanks, Riley," I said, putting on a huge smile. "Where should I go, and when?"

"Just come to the gym right after sixth period. After practice, I'll introduce you to everyone."

At 3:10 p.m., I opened the door to the gym. No one was there. I got out my reporter's notebook. It's the long, skinny kind that real newspaper reporters use. It's wire bound at the top. I'd never used one before, but my dad gave me a whole pile of them when I told him I was trying out for the *Shark*. I'm surprised he didn't give me a tape recorder and a new laptop. He was *that* excited.

The door from the girls' locker room flew open, and seven long-legged, perky girls bounced out, followed by one of the social studies teachers. The girls wore workout clothes: shorts or yoga pants, T-shirts or tank tops, and sneakers. The advisor, Ms. McDermott, was still wearing her teacher clothes.

"Okay girls, follow Shanna for the warm-up and your stretches," Ms. McDermott said. She headed off to a corner with a clipboard and a tote bag filled with notebooks.

Shanna was an African-American girl with tons of long, curly hair that was held back by a wide headband. I have to admit I was pleased that the Shark cheerleaders weren't all blonde like Riley. Another girl had straight, silky black hair and she looked like she was Asian. Two girls, besides Riley, had bright blonde hair. They were the same two girls we'd seen on the first day of school. Madison and Brittany, I thought their names were. The last two girls had kind of blondish, honey-colored hair like me. One wore it short, and the other had it pulled back in a long ponytail.

"Girls, we need to clear our heads," Shanna said. She put a CD in her boombox. Nature sounds mingled with music. It sounded like yoga music. And guess what? It was.

"Clear those thoughts, empty those heads," Shanna said in a calm, sing-song voice.

Empty those heads? Okay. No cheerleader jokes here. But I had to write that down in my notes.

"Now stretch for the stars. Deep breath in. Hold it. And exhale," Shanna made a loud huffing noise. After just three minutes, the music started getting faster. Nature sounds receded and a drumbeat picked up. Shanna led them through more yoga poses.

"Whew!" Riley said enthusiastically. The others chimed in. The music changed again. Hip-hop. The girls were moving fast and furious, following Shanna. Sweat was dripping.

"Okay! That's great! Let's take a break and get some water!" Shanna said after about twenty minutes.

Brooklyn and Rachel came into the gym.

"What the heck are you doing here?" Rachel asked me.

"Shhh!" Brooklyn said. "She's on a story! A hard news story on the complexities of cheerleading."

"Huh?" Rachel said.

"I'm doing this totally weak excuse of a story for the school newspaper," I said. "I'm supposed to cover the varsity cheerleading squad."

"It's journalistic hazing, if you ask me," Brooklyn said.

"What do you mean?" Rachel asked.

"She's the freshman on the newspaper, so they're initiating her with the worst story assignment possible," Brooklyn said. "It's like fraternity hazing at college, when they make the new guys do all the totally embarrassing stuff and make complete fools of themselves. Oops. Not that you'll make a fool of yourself or anything."

I decided to let that one slide. "What are you guys doing here?"

"We have to pick up the paperwork to be on teams," Rachel said.

"You guys? On teams? Which teams?" I asked.

"Just in case," Brooklyn said quickly. "You know, just in case we decide to try out for some team or another. Like lawn bowling or yard darts. Or volleyball. We'll have all the paperwork ready."

Brooklyn Cicero had been the star volleyball player at Middletown Middle School. She didn't need to pussyfoot around it.

"But volleyball season is months away," I said.

"I just wanted to get it out of the way," Brooklyn said.

The cheerleaders had gathered back after their water break. "Back to work for me, guys," I said, making a show of whipping out my reporter's notebook and Hello Kitty pen.

Brooklyn and Rachel headed over to the activities office outside the gym. There was some guy hanging out behind the bleachers. I wondered if he was there to gawk at the cheerleaders. Ewwww!

Then I noticed it was Sam Benson! He saw me and kind of waved before heading out to meet up with one of his skateboard buddies. He looked embarrassed. What was he doing there? ICK! Was Step-Sam following me?

Stomp, clap-clap. Stomp, clap-clap.
Step, back! Out of our way!
The Sharks are here to send you away!
Stomp, clap-clap. Stomp, clap-clap.

You guessed it. The cheerleaders were back.

"Great job, girls!" Ms. McDermott said. "Now, this time, try to get your jumps as high as Riley's. Riley, can you come out front and go through this cheer, and then show us your best jump?"

Riley moved to the front.

Stomp, clap-clap. Stomp, clap-clap.
Step, back! Out of our way!
The Sharks are here to send you away!
Stomp, clap-clap. Stomp, clap-clap.

Riley sprung into the air, totally vertical as if she had a spring under her feet. Her legs spread out into a "V" and she touched her toes, landed for a millisecond on the ground, and then was up in the air again for a second toe-touching "V."

She *was* good. I felt bad for doubting that she was good. Because Riley was beyond good. She was a fabulous dancer with a combination of precise moves and rhythm. And I've never known anyone who could jump that high.

She stopped, turned around, and smiled at the girls. Shanna clapped and smiled. Brittany (one of the other blonde girls) scowled. Madison (a clone of Brittany, only two inches shorter) bent down to adjust her shoe. The others just stared.

"Okay," Shanna said. "That's enough for today. Don't forget, everyone, tomorrow night's our first game. We'll meet here at 6:15 and then take the team bus to Eastside

High. Now, anyone want to go with me to Saturn to get something to eat? I'm famished!"

The girls nodded their heads.

"Anyone need a ride?" Riley asked. "I have room in my car for four."

"That's okay. I think we already have it all figured out," Madison said, turning on her heel. "Come on, girls." The rest of the team followed Madison into the locker room.

This seemed to diminish Riley's spirit for about a nanosecond. She turned around and caught my eye.

"Carmen!" Riley rushed up to me. "Want to come with us? I can give you a ride."

I never turn down a chance to go to Saturn.

"Okay, thanks. That'd be great. I just have to call my mom," I said.

"You can use my cell. Call her on the way."

Saturn has incredible burgers and the world's best onion rings, plus thick, huge milkshakes (one shake serves two to four). It's cheap and good. They play great music and they play it just loud enough that you can always feel the beat. The place was almost full, but the dinner rush hadn't hit yet. I followed Riley to a corner booth. She slid in and motioned to me.

"This is my stepsister, Carmen Bernstein," Riley said. "She's a freshman."

Shanna said "hi" and smiled at me. The others just kept talking. I guess I'm going to need to develop a thick skin for this reporting stuff. I reminded myself that I had a job to do.

"Carmen's doing a story for the school newspaper on us," Riley said.

"That's great!" Shanna said, chomping on a french fry. "I'm the captain, so you can ask me anything you might want."

"I'm mostly just observing your practices, but maybe you could tell me about how you work out to get ready for cheerleading. What did you have to do this summer to prepare for the year?"

In a flash, all the attention switched to me. I was the most popular girl at the table.

"Gosh, Carla," Madison said. "You wouldn't believe how hard I trained this summer."

"Me, too!" Brittany gushed. "My dad said it was like I was trying out for the Olympics. I, like, got up before ten every morning and did six miles on the treadmill before my Pilates class."

"Yeah, and both of us had weekly massages to keep our muscles supple," Madison chimed in. "People underestimate how hard cheerleading is on the body.

We really have to pamper ourselves to keep going."

"It's true!" Brittany said. "All the jumping is murder on my feet. They should give cheerleader discounts at the Nail Shoppe, since we all needed pedicures every few days." The others laughed. Riley laughed loudest.

"Some of us just run and stretch to keep in shape, and then paint our own toenails," Shanna said quietly.

I liked her. But her comments didn't seem to register with the rest of the table.

"As a team, we need to emphasize uniformity in our appearances," Madison said. "That's why Brittany and I had the exact same highlights put in our hair this summer."

They both moved their heads and flipped back their hair, letting the shiny blonde splendor catch the light. At least, that was the desired effect.

"We had David at The Hair Palace put in both lowlights and highlights," Brittany went on, still flipping her hair. "It's a combination of 'summer wheat' and 'Hollywood lights.' David made a masterful mix." Brittany looked at me expectantly. I dutifully made some notes in my reporter's notebook. Wouldn't want to miss out on that masterful mix.

"Not all of us could use blonde highlights, though," interrupted Katie Wong, who held up a hunk of her shiny dark hair. "So we booked French manicures together at

Frenchy's." Madison, Brittany, Liza, Morgan, and Katie—
five of the seven cheerleaders—held out their hands.
Gosh, I must not be a very observant reporter, because I
hadn't even noticed that their fingernails were the exact
same color of a frosty purplish-pink.

"It's called Heather Frost," Brittany said. "Isn't it just
delish? I'm going to name my first daughter Heather
Frost."

"On that note, it's time for me to jet," Shanna said.
"My calculus homework is calling."

"Me, too. Only it's my mom calling me, reminding
me that I'm tutoring my neighbor tonight," said Liza,
flipping her cell phone closed. The table was silent as
Shanna and Liza headed out.

"They're such brainiacs," Madison said with a tone
of amazement.

"Yeah, but they're still super good-looking and
popular, not to mention coordinated," Brittany said.

They moved on to making jokes about their parents and their fuddy-duddy neighbors, while I stared at
the door. There were Brooklyn and Rachel walking in
with Brooklyn's mom. Rachel started walking toward
me, and then she froze in her tracks when her eyes
took in who was at my table. Her eyes got big and she
turned her face into a look of fake horror. She backed
up dramatically.

I couldn't help it, I laughed.

"Oh, I know!" Riley said to me. She must have thought I was laughing at what she said.

"I miss my real dad so much," Riley went on, turning her attention to the group. "My stepdad is nice and everything. But he's a total dorkmeister."

What? Riley was talking about David Bernstein. *My* dad.

"He tries to be cool and to talk with us, but he's a newspaper reporter, for goodness sake. How uncool is that? He doesn't even make much money." Riley laughed. "And he's always saying stuff like: 'If I don't watch my weight, I'll start looking like a big old Polish sausage.'"

She said the last part in a goofy voice that sounded nothing like my dad.

I was stupefied. Why was she making fun of my dad? And in front of me? If this is the way she talked when I was around, what kinds of things did she say when I was not? I was shaking.

"I have to go. My mom's working at the library now, and if I hurry I can get a ride home with her," I said.

And I flew out of Saturn. Away from Riley.

My blog was calling me. I could post when I got to the library.

The Mobile Blogger
Thursday, September 9

I'm looking for an extracurricular activity. One that will make me immediately popular. Drama club? Chess club? School newspaper? Cheerleading? Which do you think will get me the most dates?

Not so tough a question. This is the twenty-first century and we still worship cheerleaders. Even if we think they're kind of silly. If you're a girl, there might be a part of you that thinks it would be fun to jump and yell and have people idolize you. If you're a guy, you know that your social stock would climb immediately if you dated a cheerleader.

Look at our own beloved MHS. A girl from West Valley High transfers to our school and joins the cheerleading squad. Never mind the fact that you can't do a proper pyramid with seven people. (Think about it.) She's accepted and boom! Instant popularity.

But what exactly is it that makes someone popular? Nice manners and kind actions? Or good looks and an "I make fun of you behind your back, but I'll still smile at you" attitude?

You decide.

Comments

We don't have a chess club. But we should. If anyone else is out there and is interested, let's meet after school tomorrow at the Activities Office. We can start our own.
posted by Square Pi, September 9, 7:25 P.M.

I don't want to be a cheerleader. But I want to play chess. Meet you guys there.
posted by T-Bone, September 9, 7:26 P.M.

I'll be there, too. Chess is cool. I feel popular already.
posted by Woofer, September 9, 7:28 PM

Will The Mobile Blogger be there? Will there be processed cheese?
posted by WriterGrrl, September 9, 7:35 P.M.

I'll bring some processed cheese and my board. My chess board, that is. It goes without saying that my skateboard will be there.
posted by T-Bone, September 9, 7:38 P.M.

Chapter 5

"Did you read The Mobile Blogger last night?" Brooklyn asked. We met on the side steps before we went into school each morning.

"The what?" I asked.

"Oh, come on! You can't fool me!" she said.

"I can't?" I squeaked. Ohmygosh. Did she know my secret?

"I know you read it," Brooklyn said. "Everyone is reading it. Unless, of course, your social life is just too busy for reading blogs, now that you hang out with cheerleaders and jocks."

"Oh, come on! I wasn't hanging out with them," I said. "I was on a hot story." Then I told her about how Riley had a total personality change midway through the afternoon and started being mean about my dad.

"That's horrid," Brooklyn said. "No one should

make fun of your dad, except you, of course,"

"You'd think that would be a right protected by the Constitution," I said, taking on a gruff lawyer voice. "One can make fun of one's own parents, but no other person will be tolerated doing such."

Brooklyn laughed. "Right. Anyway, back to the TMB, you know, The Mobile Blogger. So did you read it?"

I looked down. "I was busy last night. I had to work on my article for the *Weekly Shark*. I have to turn it in to Elliott today after school."

"Elliott Goodman?" Rachel had joined us. "He's so-o-o-o cute. And I love that he's a reporter. Kind of like Clark Kent."

"I don't think Elliott is really all that much like Superman," I said.

"Not Superman," Rachel said. "Superman is too muscly and wears too much Lycra. His cape bugs me. Clark Kent is the hottie. A smart guy who can think and write."

I have to admit that Elliott is pretty darn good looking. But I had no idea that other people thought he was cool. The editor of the school newspaper? I checked the sign above the door.

Yep. It was still Middletown High. But it was starting to feel like an alternate universe.

"Hey, Carm, how come you didn't try out for swim

team?" Rachel asked. We were walking up to the third floor to our lockers.

I probably should have told her right then about my diving problem, but I don't know, I just couldn't. I was too embarrassed. So, I came up with something even better. "Remember, I don't like organized sports any-more . . ."

" . . . only disorganized sports," Rachel and Brooklyn finished for me.

"Something like that," I said. "Besides, I have my hair to think about." I did my best Mall-O-Rama Girl voice.

"Right."

"No, really," I said. "Chlorine wreaks havoc on curly hair. It's like my hair is a sponge, and it just absorbs all the chemicals and then turns into a frizz-muffin."

"But you swim almost every day," Brooklyn said. As my best friend, Brooklyn knew almost everything. For instance, she knows that I'm kind of vain about my hair. I have great hair. Shoulder length, kind of dark golden, super shiny, with this natural wave in it. Before I cut it in seventh grade, Brooklyn used to tell me I had goddess hair.

"And I'm a total slave to my hair because of swim-ming," I said. "I have to wet it and put this special conditioner on before I put on my swim cap. And then I have to use a deep conditioner after I swim. It's a big deal. And I don't want to have to do it every morning before school. Especially not at 6 a.m."

"I don't want to do anything at 6 a.m.," Rachel said.

"Especially not get in an icy cold pool," Brooklyn added.

"Especially with the boys swim team at the same time," I added.

"It's not *that* cold," Brooklyn said. "Sometimes you just have to dive in."

The bell rang. Five minute warning. We had 300 seconds to get to first period.

I passed Riley in the hall after school. I know that she saw me, but she looked away first. I had no choice but to do the same. What's with her? She acts all nicey-nice to me one day, and then she's a jerk to me the next.

Then I forgot about her. I had to get to my locker in the next five minutes so I could turn in my cheerleading story before the deadline. On my way, I passed Sloan, the music and drama critic from the *Shark*. She was pulling a jar of Watson's CheeseStuff out of her locker. She held it up for her two friends. One of them pulled a box of crackers from her backpack.

Finally, I reached locker number 392. Brooklyn,

Rachel, and Nova were gathered around. At least they would be normal.

Or maybe not.

"Look at this," Rachel said. "Little snack-sized packs of processed cheese. And it's good." She passed them out.

"What's with all this processed cheese fascination all of a sudden?" I asked.

"Carmen! Come on! Get with it. The Mobile Blogger started obsessing about processed cheese. It's kitschy now," Brooklyn said.

"Very retro," Nova added.

"It's gross," I said. I grabbed my disk and hightailed it to Ms. Neimo's room.

"This is just great, Carmen," Ms. Neimo said. "Save it to the file that says '09.13_issue' and I'll make sure it gets to Elliott for editing."

"Do you have another assignment for me?" I asked.

Did I make the cut to be on the staff is what I really meant.

"Don't worry. You'll be a permanent staff member," Elliott said, walking in behind me. "I already added your name to the staff list in the masthead. But I'm not making assignments for the next issue until our meeting next week. See you here Monday after sixth period."

I headed out, with a big smile on my face.

I, Carmen Bernstein, star reporter in pursuit of the truth, was on my way to winning the Pulitzer Prize. Maybe not for this story, but surely for something else.

I cut through the main lobby on my way out. The lobby is a big scene before school and between classes, so I usually avoid it. The juniors and seniors have staked their claim to "The Lobby." But this time of day it would be empty. I mean *should be.*

I counted eight small groups of people clustered around chess boards.

Step-Sam looked up from one and waved. Brooklyn was there, too!

"What's up?" I asked.

"It's a chess sit-in," Brooklyn said. "Last night, The Mobile Blogger started talking about chess, so a bunch of people decided to start a chess club. We don't have an official club yet, so we're just hanging out and playing. And it's totally fun. It's like we suddenly feel like we can be cool, even though we're just freshmen."

I looked around. There were probably close to thirty people in the lobby. All kinds of kids. Even upperclassmen, but mostly freshmen and sophomores. Jocks, brainiacs, tough guys, tougher girls, nice guys, and nicer girls. You couldn't get a better cross section of Middletown High if you did a random sampling. This was cool!

"Wow!" I said. "But I can't stay. I have to go to the Steps tonight—"

Oops! I'd let "the Steps" slip out of my mouth when Step-Sam was right there.

"Going to the Steps?" Sam asked. "It's okay. You can say it. I even know that you call me Step-Sam sometimes."

I could feel my face heating up. I glared at Brooklyn, who was looking intently at the chessboard.

"Um, sorry about that," I said.

"It's okay," he said. "Really. I don't mind."

"Anyway, I want to go home first and then go over to Dad's house. I mean your house."

"I'll walk with you," Brooklyn said.

"Me too," Sam said.

Okay, now I *know* I'm in an alternate universe.

Brooklyn and I walked for a few blocks in silence. Sam trailed behind us, with his skateboard tucked under his arm. When we came to an intersection, Brooklyn halted and waited for Sam to catch up.

"Cool pool board," Brooklyn said to Sam. "Oops. Didn't mean to rhyme there."

"That's okay," Sam said. Was he blushing? "And thanks. I just built this one."

"Wow," Brooklyn said. "I've been thinking of building a custom board, too."

She had? Since when?

"I can't decide if I should get a blank deck and then paint my own thing on it, or if I should get this new one I saw at Urban-Z."

"Check it out! I was just at Urban-Z last night and they have a brand new shipment from Goat," Sam said.

"Goat is totally cool! I'd love to get a Goat!"

Huh? I could have sworn that Sam and Brooklyn both said "goat."

"Did you say goat?" I asked. I must have heard wrong. I could handle random references to "dive" in daily conversation. I was even getting accustomed to people's weird attraction to processed cheese. But I had to draw the line at "goat."

Honestly, the message from Dad's P-Com flashed into my mind, crystal clear: *Make up a cheer using the words dive, goat, and processed cheese.* I shook my head to get the image out of my mind.

"What's 'Goat'?" I asked. "I never heard of it."

"Carm, I can't believe you haven't heard of Goat," Brooklyn said. "It's a new skateboard company. They make all kinds of stuff, even clothes. I've got to go to Urban-Z and get some Goat. Then when I get a Goat deck, I can say I'm getting on my Goat."

Well, there you go. I'm pretty sure I'm in some weird alternate universe right now.

Friday night at the Steps. This was supposed to be a big Togetherness weekend, according to Dad. But guess what? As soon as I got there, Dad, Sam, and Michelle headed out the door to go watch Riley cheer at the football game over at Eastside High. They looked disappointed that I didn't want to go.

But what did they expect? After what Riley said about my dad, there was no way I was going to do the "supportive stepsister" act. Unfortunately, Mom was working until 9:30 p.m., so I couldn't go swimming either.

It was just me, Murphy, my laptop, and The Mobile Blogger.

The Mobile Blogger
Friday, September 10

I went to school at Middletown High today. At least I think it was MHS. Was I the only one who witnessed people eating processed cheese? Was I the only one who was surprised to see so many people playing chess? And now am I the only one who isn't at the MHS Shark football game at Eastside High?

I've been a freshman for only four days, but I've already learned a lot. Like, school is what you make it. If you want to hang with your friends and start a new club, you can. If you want to hang out alone on a Friday night, you can. If you don't want to be a cheerleader, you can still be a cool person.

Right?

Comments

You're not the only one not at the football game. I haven't been to one yet. And I'm a junior.
posted by WriterGrrl, September 10, 8:43 P.M.

Do you think we could get cheerleaders for chess?
posted by Saber, September 10, 9:10 P.M.

Ewwww!
posted by CharBroil, September 10, 9:11 P.M.

Chapter 6

Sunday morning, I was sitting at the kitchen counter eating a bowl of Quisp and reading the comics when Dad came in to get a cup of coffee.

"That stuff will kill you," he said, motioning to my cereal.

"Not if I keep swimming," I said, taking another bite of Quisp. "Speaking of which, will you give me a ride to Aqua Dive this morning?"

"I'll do something better than that," Dad said.

Riley burst in through the back door, already back from her morning jog. "Hi sleepyheads!" she said, snatching the comics from me.

"Riley," Dad began.

Hey! Cool! He was going to yell at her for taking the comics from me. In my house, no one ever messes with the comics before I read them. I read every single one.

Even the super lame ones like *Family Circus* and the old-fart ones like *Sally Forth* and *Funky Winkerbean*.

But no-o-o-o-o . . .

"Could you get your brother down here?" Dad asked Riley.

"I'm here," Step-Sam said. He snatched the comics from Riley and sat at the end of the counter.

I snatched them back from him. I hadn't gotten to *Zits* or *Rover* yet.

"I have some great news for all of you," Dad said. He reached into the kitchen desk drawer and pulled out two small cards. "I'd like to present you with your own Aqua Dive memberships."

Dad was grinning ear to ear.

"Wow! That's great. I really need a fifty-meter pool," Sam said. I'd never heard so much excitement come out of his mouth.

"Well," Dad said. "Carmen and I enjoy swimming there so much, I thought we all should be able to swim together."

Michelle came in the kitchen and put her arms around Dad's waist and gave him a big squeeze. I wanted to give him a big squeeze, too—right around the neck.

Aqua Dive was for *my* family. For Mom, Dad, and me.

"Riley," Dad said. "I thought maybe you could give Carmen a ride to the pool this morning. She looks like she's having water withdrawals."

I *was* having water withdrawals. I hadn't been swimming for thirty-eight hours. But I think the barfy look on my face meant something else right then.

"Sure, I guess," Riley said. "Thanks, David, for the membership. That's really nice of you." She tucked the card in her pocket. "I'll go get my stuff. Meet you at the car, Carmen."

I gritted my teeth. The last thing I wanted to do was spend the morning at the Aqua Dive with my psycho stepsister. But Dad was beaming.

I had no choice. I nodded.

Sam snatched the comics.

Argh!

This was only the second time I'd been in Riley's beast of a machine. I thought her '64 Plymouth was cavernous the first time, but now it was clear no car would be big enough to provide enough space between me and Riley Benson. I sat so close to the door I was practically hugging it, like I was a kidnap victim trying to escape.

"Hold on!" Sam came racing out of the house with

a gym bag. "I'm going, too." He opened my door and I started to tumble out. I recovered with about as much dignity as an orangutan and then moved over, so he could climb into the backseat.

Riley backed out. Talk about an uncomfortable silence. No one said anything.

"This is an . . . interesting car," I said.

"Even though it is a gas-guzzler, you mean?" Sam said.

"I'd rather drive a small car," Riley said. "Your mom has a totally cool car. I'd love to have a hybrid."

"But this is our dad's baby," Sam sad.

"Sometimes it feels like he cares more about this car than he does us," Riley said. "He made a really big deal out of giving it to us the day before school started. You can't imagine how embarrassed I was to go to a new school in a huge old car like this."

"Try being the passenger in this huge old car on the first day of school, with your sister the cheerleader driving it," Sam said.

When we got to the pool, I showed Riley and Sam how to check in and pointed Sam toward the men's locker room. Luckily, the front desk guy gave Riley and me lockers two rows apart, so I didn't have to change right next to her. There's nothing worse than making small talk while you're changing clothes.

The pool wasn't too busy. It was about half serious lap swimmers and half people just messing around. Sam was on the rope swing when we first got out there.

"Hey, Riley, dive in from the high dive," he said when he came back to the water's surface.

"You got it," she said.

I did my slip-into-the-water thing hoping that I went unnoticed by the world. I watched as Riley went up the ladder to the high dive, walked to the edge, jumped off the edge, touched her toes, and turned her head and torso down into a beautiful dive. Stunning, really. Almost like an Olympic diver.

Perfect Riley was a perfect diver, too. I should have known.

I put on my goggles and started my warm-up laps. The great thing about swimming is that the rest of the world disappears when I'm in the water. Best yet, I feel invisible. I guess if you can't see that people are looking at you, you don't know that people are looking at you, and then you feel invisible. As you might have noticed by now, going unnoticed is what I like best.

I swam hard for forty-five minutes and then rested on the edge.

"Carm, let's hit the sauna," Riley said. "I brought some great hair conditioner that intensifies in the heat."

As much as I hated to be in a small, dark room, with my psycho stepsister, she had me with the hair products. Deep conditioning my hair is almost a religious experience for me. I climbed out of the pool and followed Riley into the sauna. Luckily, no one else was there.

"I can only stay in for less than ten minutes," I said, making sure to sit close to the door in case I needed to make a quick getaway. "I get too light-headed if I stay longer."

"Me, too," Riley said. "But ten minutes is long enough for this conditioner. You won't believe how shiny it makes your hair."

I sat back, closed my eyes, and tried to relax. But all I could think about were those mean things Riley had said about my dad.

"Listen, Carmen, I'm really sorry about the other day," Riley said softly.

I didn't say anything.

"David, your dad, he's a really great guy. And he's a super stepfather. He's so nice to Sam and me."

"Then why did you tell those other girls about how dorky he is?" I tried to keep my voice from trembling.

"I'm not really sure. I don't usually let people get to me like that," Riley said. "But those MHS cheerleaders—all of them except for Shanna—they're just different from the girls I'm used to hanging out with. I want them to like me. I want to fit in. So far they haven't been liking the regular me."

I didn't say anything.

"They seem to think making fun of anyone who is smart or normal is cool," Riley said. "When Madison was making fun of her stepfather, I just thought I'd one-up her."

I opened my eyes and looked at her.

Riley hung her head. "I'm really sorry. I acted like I was one of them."

"You are one of them," I said.

"No! I'm not!"

"You're a cheerleader," I said. "And you wanted to be a cheerleader."

"Just because you like to do the same things as someone else doesn't mean that you're that same kind of person. I'm surprised that you would think that. I thought you were some kind of teenage intellectual. Do you think you're exactly like everyone on the *Weekly Shark*? Were you the same as everyone on your softball team last year? Do you think Sam's the same as everyone on the swim team?"

"No," I said sheepishly.

"Everyone knows that if you're on a team you're still

an individual. But if you're a girl and you're a cheerleader, people start assuming things about you. That you're not as smart. That you're not as deep."

I didn't know what to say to that. Because the truth is, that's exactly what I had thought.

"So now here I am at a new school," Riley went on. "I miss my friends horribly. No one knows what I'm really like. Suddenly I'm a cheerleader and they've decided who I am. I hate it."

"It is kind of unfair," I said. "Do you wish you weren't a cheerleader?"

"Sometimes," Riley said softly. "It's fun, though. At West Valley, it wasn't as big of a deal as it is here. You could be smart, athletic, normal, and a cheerleader all at the same time. But at Middletown, you basically are expected to shop and paint your toenails."

I was still a little bit mad about the way Riley had acted with the other cheerleaders, but she had a point. Besides, my head was spinning. I had to get out of that sauna. "Riley, I am sorry if I made assumptions about you. I'd love to talk more, but I'm going to faint if I don't get into a cold shower."

"Me, too," Riley said. "Let's get out of here."

The Mobile Blogger
Saturday, September 11

Being in a blended family isn't exactly those like annoying happy TV shows you see on cable family channels. It's not horrid, either, like in some of those doom and gloom books.

It's just weird. Just plain weird.

Nothing ever feels quite right. I'd kind of adjusted to my parents living in separate places. It isn't perfect, but they're polite to each other.

But then my dad got married. So now I have a stepmom. She's nice to me and everything. She tries really hard. I can tell she's trying. And she'd be perfectly fine as a neighbor or something. She's even marginally okay as my dad's wife. But I feel like now my dad has a family with her and her kids, and when I visit I'm just a guest. A guest in my own dad's house. It's so weird.

Comments

At least you don't have a stepdad too. Both my parents got remarried, so now I have a mom and a step-dragon, and a dad and a step-monster. They say I have two homes. I think I have no place that feels right. I try

to stay away from both as much as possible.
posted by WriterGrrl, September 11, 10:01 P.M.

The worst is ending up with a stepsibling your same age. It's like you suddenly have an evil twin. The only thing possibly worse is if the evil twin is a girl.
posted by T-Bone, September 11, 10:03 P.M.

Chapter 7

"You know, it's not too late to join the swim team," Brooklyn told me when we met to go to homeroom and LA-9A together on Monday morning.

"Now, why would I want to do that?"

"Maybe because you're an incredible swimmer," Brooklyn said. "Maybe because it would make my life easier."

"What do you mean, make your life easier?"

"It's not easy being your best friend every day, you know," Brooklyn said with dramatic anguish, and a creeping smile. "You can be a little high-strung sometimes, but you're way happier if you spend some refreshing, exhilarating, motivating, invigorating, calming time in the water. And if you're happier, my job as Carmen Bernstein's Best Friend gets a *lot* easier."

"So I should swim to make your life easier?"

"Ah, come on. Swim team's not that bad."

"How would you know? Are you in the water at six in the morning? Are you sharing the pool with boys in Speedos? Do you have to do whatever some coach with a whistle tells you?"

"Coach Fujita isn't that bad," Brooklyn said. "The boys aren't that bad either."

"How did you become such an expert?" I asked.

Brooklyn didn't say anything until we were almost to the door of Ms. Neimo's room.

"Because I joined the swim team last week," she said under her breath. Then the bell rang.

What????

That's what I wanted to scream. How could my best friend do something so huge, like try out for the high school swim team, and I not know about it? What kind of best friend was I? Then again, how could my best friend not know that I'm The Mobile Blogger? It seems like we'd both been keeping secrets from each other. Still, I felt hurt that Brooklyn hadn't told me. I also felt like a poor excuse for a friend that I hadn't noticed or asked her. She had been asleep a couple times last week when I'd called, and her mom had said she had to get up early. I was so worried about my problems with Riley that I hadn't thought to ask why she was getting up early.

I couldn't stop thinking about swim team, but that's

because homeroom was buzzing about the MHS Swim Sharks. They had a meet coming up that weekend, and the word was that with Sam Benson on the team, along with a few of the returning juniors and seniors, the boys' team would be first in the league. These guys could not get over themselves.

"What about the girls' team?" I asked. "How come all you guys talk about is yourselves?"

Sam looked at Brooklyn and then at me. "The girls' team is really strong too," he said. "They're down a couple of swimmers, though, and the coach is trying to recruit new swimmers. Otherwise everyone will be too exhausted because they'll be in too many events."

"People!" Ms. Neimo called from the front of the room. "Your attention please? Now today I'd like to discuss . . ."

Brooklyn passed a note to me. "Try out? Please?"

"Nope," I wrote back.

"Why not? We could have fun." She drew a cartoon of her and me in swimsuits, with goggles over our eyes and water dripping from us. It made me laugh, which, unfortunately, got Ms. Neimo's attention. She stared daggers at me.

I sat up a little straighter. Then I wrote in tiny little letters "I can't dive" and slipped it back to Brooklyn.

It was a few minutes before she sneakily put her hand

behind her back and flung the note up onto my desk.

I unfolded it to find another cartoon, this time of me doing a belly flop. I had a big smile on my cartoon face, and there were other heads bobbing in the pool smiling and cheering for me.

At the top in swirling letters Brooklyn had written: "Carmen Dives In." I laughed.

Oops. Ms. Neimo was headed for me. "Therefore the assignment will be to write a personal narrative about your experience." She barely paused. "I'll take that. Thank you."

She unfolded the note and looked at it. Sam was craning to see what was inside. Had I totally overestimated Ms. Neimo? Was she actually one of those retro teachers who believed in humiliating students? Would she make it into a bulletin board display for all her classes to see what happened to note-passing students?

She slipped the note into her pocket. Whew. I was off the hook.

"You can get this after class." She went back to writing elements of a personal narrative on the whiteboard.

I hightailed it out of Room 304 so fast that I forgot to retrieve Brooklyn's and my note. But I was back there after school for a newspaper meeting. Ms. Neimo handed the note to me without a word.

Kids filed in after school, talking about the year's first issue of the *Weekly Shark*. "Everyone's already asking me what I'm going to review next," Sloan said.

"What are you going to review next?" a guy with a pierced eyebrow was asking her.

"I like to keep things on the Q.T. so that my voice has maximum impact when the paper comes out," she said.

She opened her bag and took out a squirt can of Watson's CheeseStuff. "I come with processed cheese to share." She set it down in the middle of the conference table. Ms. Neimo pulled a box of crackers out of her cupboard and poured a bunch onto a plate. She passed the crackers and the Watson's around.

"Okay folks, one issue down," Elliott began. "We all did a great job with the first issue, but I'm sure there will be things we can do even better. Before we plan the next issue, let's do a postmortem on this one."

"Did you say postmortem, like what you do on a dead body?" Sarah asked.

"Yes, a postmortem," Elliott sounded irritated. "A newspaper is dead as soon as it comes out. These kinds of critique sessions are a bit like a postmortem, going over something that is no longer living and examining it piece by piece. I think a P.M. is an important part of the creative process."

Whatever.

Sloan turned to me and put her finger in her mouth, gagging. Then she turned back to Elliott. "Sounds great, Mr. Editor Man. Let's get postmortem-ing. Processed cheese, anyone?" She held up the plate of crackers and the can of cheese. Everyone started laughing. Everyone except Elliott.

We went through the paper, article by article, headline by headline, every photo and caption. Forty-two minutes later we got to "Meet your cheerleaders, by Carmen Bernstein, *Shark* reporter."

"Nice photo, dude," one of the guys said to Marcus the photographer.

"It was a difficult photo session, what with such un-attractive material," Marcus said. Some of the guys laughed a little, but most of the girls rolled their eyes.

"I think it's our strongest photo in this issue," Elliott said. The focus of the photograph was Riley, jumping in mid-air. Elliott kept looking at the photo and smiling.

I had unintentionally quoted Riley more than the other girls, mostly because I couldn't bear to talk about nail polish and hair highlights. Riley and Shanna had talked about their physical training and dance backgrounds, as well as how they studied sports so they could understand them better. Riley also talked about how a cheerleader's job was to help the crowd support the team—not to get noticed.

"The headline is bo-o-oring," Sloan said. I wanted to

point out that an editor, not the reporter, is the one who writes the headlines. But I'm sure everyone there already knew that. "The article actually isn't half bad," Sloan went on. "I mean, it's a totally lame and old-fashioned subject. In fact, even the idea of having females serve as dancing pep machines for male-oriented sports is disgusting and twenty years dead."

"They cheer for female sports as well," Elliott said, a little defensively, I thought.

"Anyway, it didn't just focus on the popularity angle. It read more like a sports article talking about the workouts and practices they do," Sloan finished.

She squeezed the letter *S* onto a cracker with the Watson's CheeseStuff while she was talking. She popped the cracker in her mouth.

"Interesting you should say that," Elliott said, "because our next assignment for our rookie reporter Carmen is a sports feature."

I couldn't help it. I moaned out loud.

Sloan turned and mouthed "Sorry!" to me.

"On that note, here are the assignments for the next issue." Elliott passed out the assignment sheets and production schedule.

I scanned it quickly to find my name. And then I found it: Carmen Bernstein: Sports feature on the Swim Sharks.

This time I moaned inwardly.

The Mobile Blogger
Monday, September 13

I'm happy to report that I've got the high school logis-
tics under control. I know where all my classes are. I
can get in and out of my locker in less than thirty-four
seconds. I have an acceptable peer group. I have a
place to hang in The Caf (and I know to call it The Caf
instead of lunchroom or cafeteria). Homework isn't
any harder than middle school, contrary to what all
our teachers told us last year. ("Just wait until you're
in high school" was a standard line last spring as
teachers loaded us up with assignments.)

I think I'm going along just fine, and then I get
thrown into a situation where I feel totally like a fish
out of water. Or, should I say in this case, a shark out
of water?

Comments

If you want to be a shark IN the water, try out for swim
team. Six o'clock. In the morning.
posted by T-Bone, September 13, 9:22 P.M.

Chapter 8

That night, I called my dad to give him the dreadful news about my reporting career. Second week on the job and I'd been relegated to a sports feature.

"What a great opportunity!" Dad said enthusiastically.

This was not the response I expected from David Bernstein, super intellectual and political reporter, someone who glanced at the sports section of the paper only because the weather forecast was on the back of the section.

"Dad!" I said. "Were you even listening to me? First I have to write about cheerleaders. A total fluff piece. And now I'm writing a sports feature. I want to cover issues!" I said.

Then it occurred to me: David Bernstein was digging the fact that my first two assignments had something to do with his new stepchildren. In his twisted brain, this was a great family accomplishment.

Actually, it turns out that wasn't what was on Dad's mind.

"I know it sounds crazy, but some of the best writing in a newspaper is in the sports section," he said.

I sighed.

"Wait! Hear me out. We talked about this when I was in college, in journalism school. Political reporters have to be objective and report both sides equally, no matter what they believe. But sports reporters can write loose. They don't have to worry that someone will accuse them of not being objective. Because it's just assumed that sports writers will gush about their home team."

"I thought you didn't read the sports section," I said.

"Sometimes I read it when I'm at work. But when I was starting out, I read it religiously. You can really learn a lot from some of the sports writers. Check out Kay Sharp and Martin Kuwasawa in tomorrow's paper. You'll see what I mean. They are two fine, fine writers."

"Sure, Dad," I said. "I'll check it out." I wasn't really paying attention. I was scouting out the refrigerator's offerings.

"Listen, Carmen, those swim practices are early in the morning. I volunteered to drive Sam there every day this week. If you stay over at our house for a couple of nights, you can ride to practice with him. I'm pretty sure the girls practice at the same time."

I didn't say anything.

"It might help your mom out," he added.

He had me there. Mom hated early mornings and would be unable to drive until she had at least one cup of coffee.

"Okay. Let me talk to Mom and get my stuff together."

Tuesday at 5:42 a.m. I was in the front seat of Michelle's SUV with Dad driving and Sam in the back. Dad usually drives a little two-seater hybrid that gets incredible gas mileage. (My environmentalist parents are more alike then they like to admit.) Mom says she knew the marriage was going to end when Dad came home with a car that held only one passenger. "There isn't any room for the dog," she said. What she was really saying was that there wasn't any room for us to be a family in that car. And maybe that meant there wasn't any room for us to be a family in Dad's life.

My parents separated when I was in the sixth grade. Not the best time to turn my world upside down, I might add. I wasn't exactly filled with self-confidence when I was eleven and twelve. Heck, I'm not confident now at fourteen.

Dad moved to an apartment closer to work. (Mom always said he was married to journalism.) Everything was reasonable and friendly, just as I'd expect from Bridget and David. However, there was no rule that I had to feel reasonable. Or act reasonable. I didn't know who to blame. Neither one of them was having an affair. Neither one was cruel. That made it even harder. I decided to take it out on both of them for my entire sixth grade year. I cringe when I look back on it. I was a total brat, acting like some spoiled, self-absorbed kid on a one-hour TV family drama.

Then again, they asked for it.

Dad didn't meet Michelle until the end of my seventh-grade year. If I'd met her under any other circumstances—like if she was our next door neighbor or my Mom's friend—I'd really like her. But, you know. You can't *like* your stepmom. I pride myself on being polite and friendly to her, without letting her into my life. Mom says I'm lucky to have an extra adult who cares for me. "Sometimes you're going to need someone to talk to, and you won't want to talk to your dad or me," she's said, more than once. Michelle's okay, but I wouldn't call myself "lucky."

I was lost in all these thoughts the entire trip. So

when Dad pulled up to the Aqua Dive, I was kind of surprised. I'd completely forgotten that for the next two weeks the city pool, where the swim team usually practices, was having a mechanical update. The high school swim workouts had moved to my pool.

At least it would be familiar territory.

"Do you want a ride to school, or are you going to walk today?" Dad asked. It was only eight blocks to the school, and it was a gorgeous day.

"We'll walk," Sam and I said at the same time.

"Do you want me to introduce you to Coach Fujita?" Sam asked, as we pushed through the door.

"That's okay. I'll go straight to the pool deck and introduce myself. Ms. Neimo already cleared it with him that I'd be watching. But thanks."

Sam nodded and headed left into the men's locker room. I cut through the women's locker room and out to the pool. The smell of chlorine filled my nose.

I love that smell! I know it's overpowering and chemical and most people don't like it. But to me it smells clean and refreshing. I get excited when I smell it, because I know I'm about to be immersed in water.

Not this time, though. It felt totally geeky to be wearing jeans, a sweater, and shoes at an indoor pool. It also felt hot. I whipped off my sweater (don't worry, I had a shirt on underneath) and tied the sweater around my waist.

"Coach Fujita?" I asked a man with a clipboard and stopwatch. He looked like he was in his twenties. He was barefoot and wearing Hawaiian print shorts, a Riki's Surf Shack tee shirt, and a whistle on a chain around his neck.

"Yep," he said, without looking up from his clipboard.

"I'm Carmen Bernstein. I'm writing a story for the school newspaper about the swim team?" Geesh. I hate it when my voice goes up at the end of a sentence like that, so it sounds like I'm asking a question. I was going to have to work on developing a Reporter Voice.

"Right. Nice to meet you, Carmen," he held out his hand to shake mine. "I need to get today's workout posted."

"Okay, thanks."

Coach Fujita went over to the whiteboard on the wall and began copying a workout from his clipboard. "But I can talk while I write," he said.

"Great!" I took out my notepad.

TUESDAY - SWIM SHARKS' WORKOUT
1,000 warm-up
5 x 100; push these!

"I vary the workouts throughout the week, but there are some standards. We always start with a thousand-meter warm-up." Coach Fujita looked over his shoulder at me. "Do you know much about swimming? Like, this is a fifty meter pool?"

"Sure," I said. "My family swims here."

"Well, good," he said. "Then you know that fifty meters is one lap. A hundred meters is down and back one time. Or two laps."

I nodded, pretending to take notes. But the truth was I already knew this stuff.

Coach Fujita went on, "So a thousand-meter warm-up means twenty laps, whatever style you want."

"And '5 x 100' means swim ten laps," I said.

"Right!" Coach looked at me with a bit more interest, as if trying to telepathically evaluate my swimming ability. "You know, we need more girls on the team. You can try out any time. We'd love to have you."

"Um, I don't know . . ." I started. I couldn't tell Coach Fujita about my diving problem. Could I?

Brooklyn came out from the locker room, still tucking her mass of thick, unruly hair into her swim cap. She saw me and gave a goofy wave. She pulled her goggles into place and then dived in, perfectly.

"Nice dive, Brooklyn!" Coach Fujita called.

My stomach flipped.

I looked at the coach. "I don't think swim team is for me."

"Suit yourself," he said. He went back to writing the workout on the board.

I copied it down into my notes, but not for the story. I was going to try it that night when I came back to the Aqua Dive with Mom.

Coach Fujita walked away, telling a swimmer in lane four to cut into the water with his hand at a sharper angle.

I took some notes on how the workout was going and the kinds of things the coach said. He had a nice manner. Even if he was correcting someone, it sounded encouraging and helpful, not at all humiliating. He *was* yelling, but he kind of had to, considering his swimmers were under water and he needed to get their attention occasionally.

After about twenty minutes, I was itching to get in the water. This was torture! I wanted to swim so badly that my body felt all twitchy.

If I was on swim team, I could push myself. I could get better and better. I could even test myself against the clock. I couldn't believe it, but I wanted to be a part of everything that was going on that morning with the team.

I visualized myself in the water, counting out laps,

doing flip turns, and pushing myself off from the side of the pool with my feet.

Then I imagined diving in.

My daydream turned to a nightmare.

Sam was the first boy to finish the workout. He stayed in the water, breathing hard, resting. Since he was the first to finish, I guess he'd be the first one I'd interview. I crouched down at the end of the lane and asked him some pretty basic questions: "What do you think about when you're swimming laps? Do you ever lose count?"

I probably didn't need to take notes. He answered everything exactly the way I would. He clearly loved to swim. I moved on to a couple other swimmers, asking some of the same questions. I figured I'd interview Brooklyn while we walked to school.

I waited out front for her. Sam came out first.

"I can teach you to dive, you know," he said softly.

I stared at him. How did he know? Who told him?

"Hi, guys!" Brooklyn came out from the community center, looking all clean and fresh. "What are you talking about?"

The Mobile Blogger
Tuesday, September 14

Can you keep a secret? I'm pretty sure I can. But maybe not. Because when I have my own secret, I eventually feel compelled to tell my best friend. It's part of the Best Friend Code that once you hear a secret, it never goes any farther. Right? I mean that's the way it's supposed to be.

But maybe that's not how it really works. I had a secret. I told my best friend. Now someone else— someone she doesn't even know that well—knows my secret. If that third person knows, who else knows?

What makes us tell other people's secrets? Do we twist them into funny little stories when there's a lull in the conversation? Do we begin by saying, now, you can't tell anyone else, because this is Top Secret?

Right now I don't feel like telling my secrets to anyone. Or hearing anyone's, for that matter. It's too much responsibility.

Comments

Well, TMB, you're becoming a total hypocrite. Because you're dishing secrets all over the Internet with your

blog, but you're keeping your identity a secret. What's with that???
posted by WriterGrrl, September 14, 9:32 P.M.

Since we don't know who you are, why don't you just tell us your secret?
posted by T-Bone, September 14, 9:55 P.M.

Chapter 9

"**J** swear on my CD collection that I didn't tell anyone," Brooklyn told me the next day.

"Not even Sam?"

"Of course not! When I say no one, I mean no one."

How, then, did Sam know I couldn't dive? I can't imagine that my mom would have told him. I don't think my dad knows. It was a mystery.

I walked to the Steps' house after school to wait for my dad. Dad called Wednesdays "our" night, which usually meant he and I went out to dinner and then hung out for awhile.

I sat down at the kitchen table and finished my math homework. I could hear Step-Sam upstairs. I just hoped I wouldn't have to see him.

"Hi, Carmen!" Michelle came in through the kitchen

door connected to the garage. She tossed her keys onto the counter and dropped her tote bag on a stool.

"Sam!" she yelled upstairs. "You need to listen to messages when you get home. There are three messages waiting." She started playing them back. "How hard is it to push 'play' and take down messages?" Michelle grumbled. The first two messages were for Riley. Then came my dad's voice.

"It's David. I've been called to an editorial and design meeting. I'm afraid I'm going to miss my dinner date with Carmen. Sam, when you get home from school, can you tell Carmen?"

"Well, I guess you didn't get that message," Michelle said. "Sorry, kiddo," she added softly.

I tried to hide my disappointment. "It's okay. I'll call my mom to pick me up. She has to work at the library tonight, but if I call her now, maybe I can catch her before she leaves."

"Oh, why don't you just stay for dinner with us," Michelle said. "And I'll give you a ride home afterward."

I shrugged.

"Carmen, really. I'd like it if you stayed for dinner. We're just having pasta and a salad. No big deal." It seemed like she was going to say something more. I bet she was on the verge of something like "and I'd like to get to know you better."

The truth is, I kind of do like Michelle. It's just still weird to me that my dad is married to someone who isn't my mom. Totally weird.

But Michelle looked so excited. And I was starving. A little Step-time couldn't kill me. I sighed.

"Okay. That would be nice," I said. "Is it okay if I hang out in the living room with my laptop before dinner?" They had one of those houses where no one actually lives in the living room. All the activity is in the back of the house, where the family room and kitchen are. "I'm working on a story for the *Shark*."

"Of course. Make yourself comfortable. We'll give you some peace and quiet." Michelle said.

I snuggled up in an overstuffed chair and put my feet up on the ottoman. Usually when I say "I'm working on a story," I'm actually blogging. But tonight I really was working on a story about the Swim Sharks for the *Weekly Shark*.

And get this: I was into it. Totally into it. I couldn't believe that I'd think it was fun to write about sports or jocks. But here was a sport I totally understood and could relate to.

I was five hundred words into my story when I heard a weird snuffling noise outside the window. I heard it again.

I looked outside and saw Riley sitting on the porch swing. There! The weird noise happened again. Was Riley crying? What could possibly be wrong in the life of the perfect Riley Benson? Maybe it was just allergies. I went back to my story.

The snuffling was getting louder and phlegmier, if you know what I mean. Like when someone's really choked up and really crying, and all these fluids are coming out of their eyes and their nose. The *real* kind of crying. The unattractive kind. I tried to ignore it.

I turned back to my screen.

Make up a cheer using the words dive, goat, and processed cheese.

I practically screamed!

Now my computer was infected. This was too much. Riley had obviously been monkeying with it. And this was the last straw. I wasn't going to stand for this anymore.

I stormed out to the front porch to confront her.

"Oh, gosh, sorry if I bugged you, Carmen," Riley said. Her face was pink, her eyes were puffy and red, and her hair was a mess. "I forgot you were in there working."

"I *was* working, Riley. And a weird message came onto my screen. Have you been using my laptop? Have you touched it at all?" My voice was wobbling a bit, I was so angry.

"I haven't gone near your precious laptop," Riley snapped. "Geesh! I've got other things on my mind."

She started crying so hard she was practically hyperventilating.

I didn't want to feel sorry for her. But she looked so miserable. Her response had been so immediate that it seemed truthful. Maybe she wasn't the culprit behind my dive, goat, and processed cheese mystery.

Gosh darn it! I was starting to feel sorry for her. Something was obviously very, very wrong in Riley Benson's world.

Ah, heck. I could feel my rage seeping out like a slow leak in a balloon.

I sat down next to her. "Riley, what's wrong? Do you want to talk?"

"I don't know," she said. "My life is such a mess right now. I don't even know where to start or what to do. I can't believe this is happening."

"What's happening?"

"They're trying to kick me off the cheer squad," she moaned.

"What? Who's trying to kick you off? Can they do that? How can they make a big deal of getting you on, and then try to kick you off two weeks later?"

"Ms. McDermott said there have been complaints from some of the girls who tried out last year and didn't make it. She said only a couple of people said anything at all, and then there was your article in the *Shark* and I guess some of the girls thought I got too much credit and attention. And then things got even worse because of that blog. You know, The Mobile Blogger?"

I nodded. Boy, howdy. Did I ever know The Mobile Blogger.

"The Mobile Blogger made a joke about how you can't do a proper pyramid with seven cheerleaders," Riley said.

"I don't think it was really a joke . . ." I said.

Riley's eyes flickered quickly, but she kept talking. "The point is that people hadn't really thought that much about there being an extra cheerleader. Or that I hadn't had to try out last spring like the rest of the girls."

"Did Ms. McDermott say you can't be on the squad anymore?"

"Not exactly. But Brittany and Madison started talking at practice about how they're not 'comfortable' with the situation. I can see everyone's point. I'm not that comfortable with it either. But I did try out at my old school and make it, and everyone acted really excited about me joining the squad." Riley sighed. "I guess it isn't exactly fair that I didn't try out against the other girls."

I had to hand it to Riley; she was good at seeing both sides of an issue.

"But the advisor asked you to be a part of it," I said. "She must have had support from the school." I took a quick breath. "Maybe they should have everyone try out again. You'd definitely make it, and Madison would be long gone."

Riley laughed, and then caught herself. She doesn't like to say mean things about her so-called "friends" on the squad.

"I *wish* it would work that way and we all had to try out," Riley said. "But, as it turns out, only I have to."

"Serious? You have to try out?"

Riley nodded. "It gets worse. Not only do I have to show I can cheer and choreograph and dance, I have to make up a 'highly original cheer' by next Wednesday. If I pass the test, I can cheer at the game next Friday."

"No sweat!" I said enthusiastically. "That's all easy stuff for you. I know you can do that!"

Look who was being a cheerleader now?

"No. I can't," Riley said. "I really can't. I can memorize. I can jump. I can dance. But I can't make something up. I'm just not creative that way. Not like you."

Me? Creative? That weird message from my computer flashed in my mind. In case you hadn't noticed, I'd been *obsessing* about it ever since that Friday before school started when I first saw it on my dad's P-Com. And the truth was I *had* thought of a cheer. It was crazy, but maybe . . . just maybe, it might work.

I stood up and cleared my throat. "How about this?"

Processed cheese, step aside.
We're turning up the heat.
Get your goat—then dive in,
Sharks don't take defeat!

Riley laughed. "That's so funny! Especially since The Mobile Blogger got people talking about processed cheese. And Sam's always talking about 'getting on his goat' and how great Goat skateboards are."

"Do you think it would work?" I asked. "Do you think it's highly original?"

"What?" Riley's eyes opened wide. "Use *that* as a cheer for my tryout? No way!"

"Come on!" I playfully punched her arm. "It would show you are in tune with what students are talking about and that you have a sense of humor. Show them that you're not afraid to laugh—or have people laugh with you!"

"Carmen!" Riley stood up and stamped her foot. "People would be laughing *at* me if I used something that ridiculous! You're trying to sabotage my cheerleading career, just like you did with your newspaper story and just like The Mobile Blogger. You think cheerleading is idiotic and so you made up the dumbest thing you could think of. You probably think I'm dumb enough to go along with it. But I'm not. I'm not dumb. And I'm not going along with it."

Riley stormed back inside and upstairs to her room.

Well, at least I had made her stop crying.

The Mobile Blogger
Wednesday, September 15

I used to think cheerleaders were total airheads. But there are some cheerleaders at Middletown High who are bright, caring, and talented. I hadn't realized how narrow-minded I was until I met some of them and read that article in the Shark. So, I was wrong. So wrong.

And now there's all this nonsense about how one girl on the cheer squad has to go through tryouts again. It seems bogus to me. Why was she invited in the first place? Then, less than a month later, why would anyone squeeze her out? Unless, perhaps—just perhaps—there's a little bit of jealousy going on.

Wait! Jealousy? Here? In high school?

Ha.

Chapter 10

"Fabulous job on your swim team feature, Carmen," Elliott said to me in the hallway. In public. In front of other people. In front of junior and senior people.

"Thanks," I said. I tried to look at him straight on, but my eyes were darting all over the place, avoiding eye contact.

"I'm thinking we'll put it on the front page for Monday's issue."

"But the paper doesn't come out until next week," I said.

"Right. Well, sometimes we try to throw people off and come out weekly. No one really pays attention. Your article came in early, and Sloan has tons of reviews for us. We've got a lot of material since it's the beginning of school, so we're going to do a special issue."

"You're going to put sports on the front page?" I asked.

"You bet. I wouldn't put football on the front page, but the Swim Sharks seem more like a thinking man's sport. Thinking woman's sport too, of course," he quickly corrected himself. Elliott Goodman would never want to be accused of being sexist in his beloved newspaper.

"That's great. The team will be psyched."

"I've got another story I want you to get on right away, before our regular editorial meeting," Elliott said.

He leaned in closer to me, wedging me up against a locker. He rested his arm up high on the locker. I wasn't sure I liked being this close to him, even though he is pretty cute. "They're making that new cheerleader, Riley, go through a special tryout next week. I think there's more to that story. How did she end up here? How did she get on the squad without trying out? I think there's a lot more to the story."

"I don't think so, Elliott . . ."

"Of course there's more to it! It's your chance to do some investigative reporting. You can really shake things up. Get to the bottom of this story about Riley. What kind of favors did she do to get on the squad? I mean, the girl's not that smart. She must have got in some other way."

"Stop it!" I said, my voice maybe a bit louder

than usual. "You're being mean and spiteful. Riley *is* smart. She's funny and she's creative. She has a lot going for her. Maybe there's something more to *your* story, Elliott? You've got something against her, don't you?"

Elliott's eyes narrowed.

A thought popped into my head. "I know . . . you're mad because she's going out with Walker this weekend instead of you!"

If we'd been in a cartoon, you'd see steam coming out of Elliott's ears right about now.

Bingo!

I'd totally guessed on that one. I knew Riley was going out with Walker. Everyone knew that. And from the way Elliott had been looking at the picture of Riley from my last story, it was obvious he had a crush on her.

"This has nothing to do with me, hotshot," he said. "I was trying to get you a big story. You could get in with the popular crowd."

Every muscle in my body was tense. I felt like I was going to explode. "Number one, I don't need to 'get in' with the popular crowd. I'm doing just fine as I am. Number two, I know Riley Benson didn't do anything unfair to get on the cheerleading squad. You're wondering how I know that? Well, I know because she's my sister, you self-centered bozo! Number three . . ."

I felt someone tap my shoulder.

"Hey, Carmen, let's get out of here." It was Sam.

I was never so happy to see someone in my life.

We were about two blocks from school before I felt like I could breathe again.

"Thanks, Sam," I said. "I guess I was getting a little carried away there."

"No, thank *you,*" he said. "Thanks for sticking up for the Benson name."

"Did you hear everything?"

"I'm guessing I heard enough. It sounds like Elliott has it in for Riley?"

I nodded. "I think he had a thing for her and she rejected him."

"Mostly what I heard was how you stuck up for her," Sam said.

I moaned. "I hope the whole school didn't hear that conversation."

"Well, not the *whole* school. Just the second floor."

My head jerked over to look at him. He smiled. "I'm kidding. I don't think anyone really heard. My ears just perked up when I heard the name 'Riley.' Then, when you said 'Benson,' I had to totally tune in. That's my name, after all."

We walked in silence for another block.

"So, what was Elliott talking about?" Sam asked.

"He asked me to do a story on the cheerleaders again, but this time to talk about Riley and how she got on the squad without trying out. I'm afraid he'll talk someone else into doing a story. It would destroy Riley. This tryout thing already has her tied up in knots."

"Wow. I didn't know you cared about my sister," Sam said.

"I kind of have to, you know, since my dad is married to your mom," I said. "And besides, I kind of want to. Riley is a nice person."

"She bugs the heck out of me," Sam said, kicking a stone down the sidewalk, sending it soaring about thirty feet. "But you're right. She is a good person."

That weekend, Mom and I went swimming both days.

"I know you think I'm not a morning person," Mom said on the drive to Aqua Dive on Saturday.

"I *know* you're not a morning person," I said. "No thinking involved."

"Granted. However, I think I can muster the strength and discipline to help get you to swim team practice," Mom said.

I winced.

"Just if you want to, of course," she hurriedly added. "I'm not saying you have to be on swim team. You're not exactly a morning bird yourself. The thing is, Carmen, you're a fabulous swimmer. You're strong. You've got good technique. And I know you love it. Don't you?"

"Yeah, I guess so," I mumbled.

"Well, just consider it. And know that if you decide to do it, you have my full support. I think I can even figure out how to program the coffee pot so it starts brewing before I get up. Maybe we could even carpool with Brooklyn's folks?"

"Okay. Thanks." End of conversation.

Wouldn't you know it? Riley was already in the pool, swimming laps. The only open lane was the one right next to her. Mom and I shared a lane and started in on our routine. Either Riley was totally oblivious to the world around her or she was ignoring me.

After our workout, Mom headed into the sauna. I went ahead and showered and headed toward my locker to change. Riley was in the same aisle. She was already dressed, but she was combing out her long straight hair.

"Processed cheese, step aside. We're turning up the heat," Riley said in a soft, sing-song voice.

I couldn't help myself. I joined in:

"Get your goat—then dive in," I said.

"Sharks don't take defeat!" Riley finished. She was looking at me and smiling.

"Caught me!" she said. "I can't get that ridiculous thing out of my head."

"Because it's so ridiculous?" I asked.

"Because it's so ridiculous that some people might actually think that it's highly original," Riley said.

"I wasn't trying to sabotage you," I said.

"I know. And Sam told me about that jerk Elliott, too," she said. "And how you stood up to him."

"Elliott's a stuck-up pseudo-intellectual loser," I said. "Don't give it a second thought. I did it for myself. It felt great to one-up him."

"Still, thanks. I appreciate it."

"No problem," I said.

"Want some?" Riley passed me a bottle of lavender lotion. "Try it. It's not too strong and it's really smooth."

"Thanks," I said. I rubbed the lotion into my legs. "This might sound totally cornball, but I want to say it anyway." I was talking fast so I didn't lose my nerve. I looked at Riley.

"The truth is I really do like you. And I would never even have considered sabotaging you or not sticking up for you. I know I'm totally uncoordinated and only a freshman, but if you'll let me, I want to help you with this tryout."

"Hey, thanks, Carm. Back at you," Riley said with a big smile.

"I still think you should consider doing something funny and unexpected," I said.

"I know. I really am considering it."

"You are?"

"I'm scared," Riley said, "but if I do something unexpected, it might show them how ridiculous the whole situation is, starting with letting me in, and then kicking me out."

"Exactly." I nodded. "You just need to take a chance."

We packed up our stuff in companionable silence. As we headed out of the locker room, Riley said softly, "You know, Carm, I was the one who taught Sam to dive."

I looked at her. How did she know?

Sam, Riley, and I instant-messaged each other until late Saturday night. We were plotting.

It's kind of funny when you think about it. Sam and Riley's rooms are about five feet apart, yet they were IM-ing each other, too.

The next morning, Mom and I headed to Aqua Dive for ten o'clock lap swim. I knew that Riley and Sam would be there at the same time. We had worked it out the night before.

Mom and I got there first, though. Mom's rotator cuff had been bugging her, so she decided to go for the hot tub instead of laps.

"I'm just going to relax my shoulder and take a long shower," she said. "I'll be hanging out in the Sports Café reading the paper and drinking coffee."

I headed into a lane by myself and did a two-hundred-meter warm-up and two hundred meters freestyle. I was resting at the edge for just a moment when Sam kneeled down.

"Ready for your diving lesson?" Sam asked.

"I'm not sure."

"Come on," Sam said. "What's the worst that could happen?"

"Let the master coach her," Riley said, coming up behind him.

Even though we'd talked it over the night before, at that exact moment I couldn't think of anything worse than diving lessons from my stepbrother and stepsister.

"Get your goat—then dive in," Riley said kindly. "Remember? You just need to take a chance."

She got me to laugh at least. Now let's see if she could get me to dive.

The Mobile Blogger
Sunday, September 19

I hate it when a parent or a teacher or a coach says "What's the worst that can happen?" They usually say it when they want you to take a chance or when you're scared to do something.

I don't know what they think the answer will be. I can usually think of some pretty horrific worst-case scenarios.

What's the worst that could happen if I asked a guy out on a date? Let's see. The guy would start laughing hysterically at the mere idea of going out with me. He'd laugh so hard that he'd choke on his gum. He'd be gasping for air and he'd fall on the floor and go into convulsions. The paramedics would arrive to carry his body out of the school. Investigators would ask for eyewitness accounts. And some busybody would come forward and say, "He was dying of laughter at the idea of going out with that girl over there."

What's the worst that can happen if you jump off a bridge? If you go bike-riding without a helmet? If you dive headfirst into a body of water?

Let's start with that last one. Where do I even begin? The water level could have been measured incorrectly, so even though you think you're heading into twelve-foot water, it's actually only three feet. The force of hitting the water could cause your swimming suit to come off in front of an entire crowd. You could get a bloody nose (that happened to me once), and it doesn't stop. Ever. For the rest of your life, you walk around with blood dripping out of one—or both—of your nostrils.

So, don't say, "What's the worst that can happen?" to me.

Because I can think of some answers.

Chapter 11

I'm not going to take you through every single diving attempt I had. Trust me when I say that it wasn't that attractive. In fact, the first few attempts were downright tragic. A couple of them really hurt because of unfortunate angles when my body entered the water. But I didn't get a bloody nose. And I had about three decent dives.

Riley was a good coach. So was Sam. They both offered tips. They encouraged me each time. They laughed when I belly flopped, but it was the right kind of laughter. Not mean.

Sunday night I dreamed about diving. Does that ever happen to you? Your body is aching to do something, and so you dream about it. You get better and better in your dream. Then, the next time you try something, you can do it better. I call it sleep visualization. I could see myself diving better. I could feel how my toes moved to get into the proper position. I could feel the strength in my torso as I willed it to stay straight. I could feel the weight of my legs, and then the weightlessness, as they went up. It was a great dream.

The dreams left me aching to dive again.

I passed a note to Brooklyn in homeroom on Monday.

"I dived in!" There was a picture of me, although not as good as the one Brooklyn drew, doing a graceful swan dive.

"Yippee!" Brooklyn wrote back.

Sam passed me a note. That was a first.

"Dive tonight?" it said. He turned and looked at me.

I nodded.

"Call us," he mouthed.

I nodded again. Brooklyn was beaming. So was I.

That night I called The Steps' house to see what time Riley and Sam wanted to meet at the pool. Dad answered the phone.

"Hey, how's my favorite female ninth grader?" he asked.

"Um, great, Dad. School's going well."

"Any more front-page stories coming out in the *Shark?*" he asked.

"Not right away. I think Elliott likes to share the wealth. He doesn't want me to get too much front-page exposure."

"I can see his point, but the best stories should be on the front page. What are you working on now?"

Ugh. How to tell Dad that since I totally dissed Elliott, he was taking it out on me by giving me the lamest assignments? My next story was on, I kid you not, sack lunches. I was supposed to do a survey on favorite items to bring in a school lunch. I had a sneaky suspicion that processed cheese was going to get mentioned a time or two.

"Well, Dad, I'm doing some investigation into school lunches," I said.

"That's a good story. There's so much you can do with FDA decisions, nutritional values, prices, and the choices bureaucrats make that can affect the health of young people." He was off, listing statistics and government offices, and offering all kinds of reporter-type tips. "You know, when Reagan was president, they tried to say that ketchup counted as a vegetable so that it would make school lunches seem more nutritious."

I hated to tell Dad that my story had more to do with whether you bring your food in a paper bag or a retro metal lunchbox. But I was about to get a twenty-year history of political decisions and debate around school lunches.

"Wow, Dad. I really like that ketchup connection. Thanks. Ketchup. Hey, I don't mean to cut this short, but I was wondering if either Riley or Sam was nearby."

"Riley? Sam? You want to talk to one of them? Hold on, I'll see who's closest."

I could tell my dad was about to burst open with happiness.

Here I was, his brilliant future Pulitzer Prize–winning daughter, reaching out to his wife's children. I hoped that neither Riley nor Sam would spill the beans about teaching me to dive. Dad would think that was just a little too perfect.

Riley came to the phone.

"Hey, Carm. You want to dive tonight? I mean, meet us at Aqua Dive?" she caught herself. I was guessing that David Bernstein, with his keenly trained reporter's ears, was close enough to eavesdrop.

"Mom and I can get there at about 7:30. Sound good?"

"See you there."

I'm not sure why I thought it was okay to tell Mom that I was learning to dive but not tell Dad. Maybe it's because swimming was one of the links that kept Mom and me in tune, even during that awful year when I was in sixth grade and I pretended I hated both of my parents. I would at least tolerate my mom long enough for her to take me to the pool.

"I'll pick a far lane and just do my workout," she said. "Carm, I'm really proud of you. But I know you'll need some space tonight."

"Thanks, Mom."

Riley and Sam were already in the water. I was about to do my little feet-first slip into the water when Riley came to the edge and grabbed my ankles.

"Not so fast, missy!" she said. "I think you're ready to dive in from the get-go."

"How about if I warm up first, and then practice diving?" I asked.

"Nope. Not this time. Dive."

And I did.

And it was . . . glorious!

I didn't belly flop. I didn't splat. I didn't flail my arms. I dived. I, Carmen Bernstein, dived in. I kept going underwater for awhile, and immediately started swimming a length and back.

"That felt so-o-o-o good!" I said when I came up. Riley and Sam were smiling.

"It does feel good, doesn't it?" Sam asked.

"Sometimes, you just got to take a chance," Riley said. "Right?"

I was still on my diving high in the locker room. It turns out Mom had seen a couple of my dives. It felt good just knowing how proud she was of me.

Riley and I headed to the soda machine in the lobby on the way out.

"Well, you took your chance," Riley said. "I guess it's time for me to take mine."

"So, does that mean you're thinking of cheering for processed cheese and goats?" I asked.

"Yep. I'm going to dive in, so to speak," she said.

"That's great! They'll never see this coming!"

"I know. I like the idea of catching them totally off guard," Riley said. "The thing is, I have only two days left. I'm kind of nervous about it."

"Seems natural to be nervous," I said.

"I feel kind of outnumbered too. All the girls on the squad will be there, judging me, along with some teachers and other students," Riley said. "So, I was wondering if maybe you and Sam would come with me. You know, for moral support."

"Come with you to the tryout? Would they let us?"

"No one said that I couldn't bring someone," Riley

said. "I'd really like to have my brother and sort-of-sister there with me."

Wow. What could I say to that? Except . . .

"Sure. I'd love to."

The Mobile Blogger
Monday, September 20

Newsflash: Life in a blended family is no longer completely miserable. In fact, it's almost okay.

Don't you just hate it when your parents turn out to be right?

My dad and stepmom are walking around with these dopey "I knew it all along" smirks on their faces. They're TOO happy, if you know what I mean. I have to act a teensy bit unhappy around them (even though it's just an act, except in the morning, when I really truly am unhappy to be up at such an unreasonable hour).

Dad always said that I'd get along "famously" with his wife's children. (That's actually what he said: "I think you'll all get along famously one day.") I wouldn't actually say "famously" is the correct word choice here. But we're getting along. And that's okay.

My life is picking up at MHS, too. It isn't exactly a

social whirl of activities, but I'm pretty busy. I barely have time to blog.

Time for a Big Deep Thought: Do people blog more when they're unhappy?

Well, I'm not saying that bloggers are losers or anything. That would be totally rude. Because if I'm a loser, then the 564 readers (at last count, not that I'm counting or anything) of The Mobile Blogger would be losers too. And I'm sure that's not true. You guys are okay, aren't you? Is anyone out there?

Comments

I'm here. Not feeling like a loser, either.
posted by T-Bone, September 20, 7:55 P.M.

Here.
posted by WriterGrrl, September 20, 7:56 P.M.

Ditto.
posted by Sk8er, September 20, 7:57 P.M.

Ditto ditto.
posted by Saber, September 20, 7:58 P.M.

Count me in.
posted by CharBroil, September 20, 7:59 P.M.

I'll go along with all of you. Although that would be more of a Beta Girl than a Gamma Girl. What are we ditto-ing?
posted by Gamma Girl, September 20, 8:01 P.M.

Huh?
posted by Woofer, September 20, 8:03 P.M.

Chapter 12

Sam passed a note to me during homeroom. "I know who TMB is," it said.

"Oh, really? Tell all." I wrote back.

No reply.

Did he really know? There was still lots of buzz about The Mobile Blogger and who it was. Now the theory was that it was a ninth-grade boy and not a girl at all. TMB was just having some fun with all of us.

I met up with Riley after school. She didn't have cheer practice, seeing as how she was temporarily kicked off the squad. I was going home with her to help her with her cheer. Now that was a laugh: Me helping someone with cheerleading. It sounds like I'm going to show her the moves or something.

I was waiting at her boat of a car when Sam came up. "You getting a ride with Riley today?" he asked.

"Yep. Is that okay with you?"

"Yeah. It's a free country. Free speech and all that. Freedom to be a secret blogger. Freedom to be The Mobile Blogger."

"Right. You said you know who it is," I said.

"I'm guessing you know, too," Sam said. "Especially since it's you."

I could have played some little game where I pretend it isn't really me, but what's the point? It is me. He found me out. It's not the end of the world.

"How did you know?" I asked.

"It wasn't that hard. I had an inkling when you started going on about processed cheese. Anthony, one of the guys on the newspaper staff, is on swim team too. He's all into processed cheese ever since the first day of journalism after school. He also told me there were two cute freshmen girls on the *Shark* staff. Being new to the school, I feel it is my obligation to find out the names of cute girls. When he said your name, I almost choked."

"Thanks a lot," I said, feeling completely depressed.

"I don't mean it that way. I mean, you're not *that* bad. But we're practically related, so it's kind of gross. You know what I mean."

I did, actually. I knew objectively that Sam was cute and cool. But, ew! He was Step-Sam.

"But what does that have to do with the Blogger?" I asked.

"I figured that there was a good chance it had to be either you or Sarah, since you're the only freshmen who would have been at the newspaper meeting that day. I followed you a bit."

"I thought you were following me! It was creeping me out. And ticking me off."

"It was just a wee bit of espionage," Sam said. "Besides, there was another reason I was hanging around."

"There was?" my voice croaked. Uh-oh. Now I was getting creeped out again. It wasn't possible that Sam had a crush on me, was it?

"It's kind of embarrassing, but I wanted to get to know Brooklyn," he said. His face was red across his cheeks.

Whew! That was a relief.

"Wow. I had no idea."

"Good!" he said. "It would have been horrible if you could tell. I hope she couldn't tell."

"What would be wrong with her knowing?"

"Well, by now she knows anyway," he said. He was a deeper red in the face now.

"We've been talking after swim practice. And we have fifth period together. Besides third, but that doesn't count because you're there and all the guys from swim team. But today in fifth, I kind of asked her to go to the Dive-In movie with me on Saturday night.

Riley swooped down to her car. "Hey, kids. Jump in. Were you guys just talking about the Dive-In movie? Are you both going?"

This Saturday the Swim Sharks were sponsoring a Dive-In movie for the whole school at Aqua Dive. The ticket sales would raise money for traveling to swim meets. I'd never been to a Dive-In movie (although I've been to a drive-in twice). You come ready to swim. The pool is full of inner-tubes and floating things. You splash around for awhile and then you float in the inner-tubes and watch a movie on the side of the wall. There were frequent "intermissions" so you could warm up and splash around and get some treats on the sidelines. It sounded so fun. I just expected that Brooklyn, Rachel, and I would go together. But it sounded like Brooklyn had plans. Wow. It was going to take me a while to get my head around that one: Sam and Brooklyn.

We got to the Steps' house and Riley went to change. Sam and I did our by-now-familiar trek to the kitchen and refrigerator to scrounge for non-nutritious snacks before Michelle got home and offered us organic produce.

"So, I'm guessing Brooklyn said yes to the movie?" I asked while I unscrewed my Oreo.

"Yeah. But Riley doesn't know. It's cool that you

didn't say anything. I don't feel like getting teased by her right now."

"But if I write about it in my blog, Riley will probably find out," I said teasingly.

Sam looked alarmed. "You wouldn't dare . . . Oh, you're kidding, right?"

"I don't want to do anything that will blow my cover anymore," I said.

"I won't tell anyone about you being The Mobile Blogger if you'll promise me one thing," Sam said.

"What?"

The Mobile Blogger
Tuesday, September 21

A few days ago I was going on and on about how someone found out one of my secrets. Well, get this: That same "someone" found out my biggest secret of all. And this time there's no chance that someone leaked the secret. Because I hadn't told anyone.

So, someone knows that I'm The Mobile Blogger. I guess it's not earth-shattering or anything. I just hope this person doesn't spill the beans.

In a way, I'm kind of glad this person found out. It's always a bit of a relief when someone knows your secrets. Then there's someone to talk to.

Let's face it. Secrets bring people closer together.
Even people you never expected to like.

Comments

You can tell me your secret. I'll meet you here tomorrow night and we can dish. Maybe no one else will
read it.
posted by WriterGrrl, September 21, 7:59 P.M.

My best friend told me a secret, and now she thinks
I told other people. There's NO WAY I'd ever do that
to friend, especially not her. She's hurt because she
thinks I betrayed her. I'm hurt because she doesn't
trust me. And I have no idea how this guy found out. I
know I didn't tell him.
posted by GoatRider, September 21, 8:04 P.M.

Chapter 13

Wednesday was tryout day. I felt nervous all day. When Ms. Neimo called on me, I had no idea what we were even talking about.

I said, "Sounds like everyone's covered it already." Luck was on my side, because no one laughed.

I met up with Sam and Riley right after school, and we headed to the gym. Riley went into the locker room to change.

"I'll let you in on a secret," Sam said while we waited for Riley.

"I'm kind of done with secrets for awhile," I said.

"That's cool. I just wanted to tell you that I'm T-Bone. You know, the T-Bone that e-mails your blog," he said.

"You're T-Bone?" I said. "I thought for sure you were Sk8er."

"Oh, I'm him, too. I'm both."

"Great. That means I have only 563 visitors to the blog," I said. We ended the blog talk when Riley came out.

"You look terrific!" I said. "Absolutely perfect. Athletic, stylish, and peppy." It's a good thing she'd decided against wearing her old West Valley High cheerleading uniform. I told her I thought that would be a little over the top. I also talked her out of shorts that said "c-h-e-e-r-s" across the butt. (What a stupid fashion statement, having writing on your butt. I mean, like, do we really need to read other people's butts? Geesh!)

Instead Riley was wearing black volleyball shorts, a yellow tank/crop top, and white athletic shoes.

"Not that you're going to need me, Riley, but I'll be there if you do," I said.

I went to the far corner of the gym. I wouldn't really be noticed there. I got out my copy of *Great Expectations*. If anyone asked, I was just doing homework and waiting for a ride home with my stepsister.

Sam's plan was to go in and out, acting like a board-head scoping out a place to skate. That way he'd be nearby if we needed him. I couldn't believe it, but I think Step-Sam was actually nervous for his sister.

The six cheerleaders were sitting like judges behind a long skinny table. Ms. McDermott was there, along with a couple other teachers and some "specially selected student leaders."

Those student leaders included Elliott Goodman. That couldn't be good for Riley. I felt like I had a ton of lard in my stomach.

"Riley, we'd like to thank you for coming today for this tryout," Ms. McDermott said. "Since you've already practiced with the squad and you know the school song, we'd like you to perform that for us now."

"Okay," Riley said. Her voice quavered. I could tell she was super-nervous.

"You can do this, Riley," I whispered, even though I knew she couldn't hear me. Maybe she'd get my telepathic message if I thought really hard. "Just ask them to start the music for you."

"Okay, here's my CD," Riley said to the panel. "I'm ready when you are. Could you please start the music?"

Shanna hit play on a boombox and a recording of the marching band playing the Sharks' theme song came on.

Riley did all the moves and jumps perfectly. She smiled the whole time. It was a good smile, though. Not one of those fake plastered-on smiles. It looked like she was having fun. The music went straight from the marching band song into a jazzy old song called "Mack the Knife."

It was totally unexpected. I could tell the judges were surprised and were groovin' to the music. The song died down.

"This is it, Riley. Processed cheese all the way," I said softly.

Riley launched into the cheer.

Processed cheese, step aside.
We're turning up the heat.
Get your goat—then dive in.
Sharks don't take defeat!

People were cracking up. It was so silly that you couldn't help but laugh.

The laughing stopped, but happy grins were on most people's faces (not Madison's, I noticed) as Riley transitioned into some gravity-defying jumps and a triple back flip.

Wow! I wanted to stand up and cheer. It was a great performance!

The judges erupted into applause. I noticed that a few weren't quite as enthusiastic, including Elliott and Madison.

"Nice job! Thank you, Riley," Ms McDermott said. "Does anyone have any questions for Riley?"

"I do," Madison said in her nasal voice. "What's the

point of that cheer, Riley? It's so ridiculous."

My stomach flipped. This was it.

"I don't know that there really is a point," Riley said. "High school is a rough, stressful time under the best of circumstances. Sometimes we just need to laugh. I think students at Middletown High School have wanted to let their guard down and not try to be so cool all the time."

She was so sincere. She didn't sound sappy at all. But I saw Madison roll her eyes.

Riley went on. "I think that's why when The Mobile Blogger started talking about processed cheese, that people started having fun with it. We all need to have a little fun. Cheerleading should be fun for those who are involved. It should help the people in the stands have fun."

Wow. That was the perfect answer.

"Thank you, Riley!" Ms. McDermott said. "Let's hear some comments from the faculty judges."

Ew! This was like some kind of star-search show where judges critique things in front of you, sometimes saying incredibly mean and spiteful things.

Ms. Neimo went first. "Riley, I think you've shown a lot of originality not just in your choreography, but also in your cheer lyrics. It shows that you have your finger on the pulse of MHS students. I like how you worked in our fad of the month with the processed cheese, included the skateboard kids with the Goat reference, and played on the Shark mascot with dive."

The other judges all nodded in agreement.

"I couldn't have said it better myself," said Ms. McDermott. "Congratulations, Riley."

One tryout down, one to go. The next one was *my* tryout.

Whoa! Don't get all fired up about it. I wasn't trying out for cheerleading. But I *was* trying out for something else. I'd promised Sam I'd do it, and in return he promised he'd keep my blog identity a secret.

"Next stop, Aqua Dive," Riley said. We all three headed to her car.

"You totally rocked, Riley," I told her. "Once you started, you didn't seem at all nervous."

"Once I started, the nervousness just went away and I was having fun. I bet it will be like that for you too," she said.

"Right now I feel like I might throw up," I said.

"Coach is a nice guy," Sam said. "You shouldn't feel nervous about him."

"I guess I'm just nervous about all the stupid things that could go wrong," I said.

I changed into my swimsuit and headed out to the pool deck.

Sam was talking to the coach. Riley was sitting on the bleachers at the side.

"Good to see you, Carmen," Coach Fujita said. "Why don't you dive in and do a quick two-hundred-meter warm-up."

He said it so casually. Just go ahead and dive in.

I took a deep breath, I put my toes on the edge, and I dived in! The worst part was over and so I just kept going. My four-lap warm-up was done in no time.

"Nice dive. Good solid stroke," Coach said. "I'm not going to time you, but I want you to do a four-hundred-meter IM."

I was off. Freestyle. Butterfly. Back. Breast stroke. The water cushioned me and made me feel secure. It was over so quickly. I pulled up to the edge to rest.

"Carmen Bernstein, welcome to the team!" Coach Fujita said. He bent down to the edge of the pool and shook my hand. "Be here at six tomorrow morning for your workout. You can sign up then to work at the Dive-In movie on Saturday."

And that was that.

I felt like I was going to burst! I leaned back into the water and let it cradle me. It was only then that I realized that I hadn't done this just to keep Sam quiet about my secret identity as The Mobile Blogger..

I WANTED this. I really wanted it. And I made it!

I jumped up and made a big splash. "Yippee!" I yelped.

The Mobile Blogger
Wednesday, September 22

I've got to start going to bed earlier. Because it's almost midnight, and that means even if I went to sleep this very second, I'd get only five hours of sleep before the five o'clock alarm goes off.

But how can I sleep? Adrenaline is pumping through my veins. I took a chance today—and it totally paid off. Forgive me, but I can't tell you the details (lest you figure out who I am), but let me just say that it is so completely and absolutely and totally worth it to take risks now and then. Want to ask someone out? Do it. Want to try out for show choir? Go ahead. Want to be a poet? Start writing.

Gosh. It feels so great to have tried something new. It feels even better that it paid off. Otherwise I'd be writing one of those "At Least I Tried and I'm Sure I Learned a Valuable Lesson That Will Build Character" kind of blog entry. Believe me, I've developed plenty of character over the past fourteen years. I'm ready to win a few challenges with all that character bursting out of me.

Goodnight. Really.

Comments

'Night
posted by T-Bone, September 22, 11:59 P.M.

Later, dude. Or dudette, as the case may be.
posted by Sk8er, September 23, 12:00 A.M.

Chapter 14

Riley made the cheer squad. I made the swim team.
But the story doesn't end there.

Saturday night, Mom dropped me and Rachel off at
Aqua Dive for the Dive-In movie. Brooklyn was going
with Sam and Riley, but it was kind of like a date. Riley
made sure she had someone else with her (Walker, the
cute, intellectual senior) so that Sam and Brooklyn both
had to sit together in the backseat.

I had ticket-selling duty but it didn't last for long.

"We're almost ready to shut down sales," Coach Fujita
said. "Looks like we have a full house. Or a full pool, as
the case may be. Why don't you close things up?"

"Be right there," I told the coach.

I was tidying up the cash box when I saw that something had fallen on the floor. Probably a quarter.

I bent down to get it. It wasn't a coin after all.

It was a small silver shark charm. I picked it up, gave it a close look. It had the shape of a blue shark. Long and sleek, the fastest-swimming shark. On the back a star was engraved into the metal. I slipped the shark charm into my pocket.

I turned back to the cash box.

"What?" I said out loud, even though no one was around. On top of the metal cash box was a large leather book with a star on it. I pulled the charm out of my pocket. It was the exact same star design.

Weird. I swear the leather book wasn't there five seconds ago. I had no idea what it was. I opened it to see if it might have a name or something inside it. But it was blank. Completely blank. Somehow I knew it wasn't supposed to be blank. It was meant to tell a story.

I picked up a pen and turned to the first page.

"Carmen, come on!" Rachel and Brooklyn stood dripping wet at the entrance to the lobby. "The movie is going to start in fifteen minutes, and we want to mess around first."

I reluctantly put the journal into a safe pocket in my workout bag and headed into the locker room to change into my swimsuit.

Brooklyn and Sam were in the water when I got out to the pool. Riley was hanging on to the side, acting all casual. But I could tell she'd positioned herself to be near the diving board. She waved me over. Sam swam over in a flash. Talk about sharks. It was like I was fresh meat and the sharks were converging to tear me apart.

"Processed cheese, step aside. Carmen's turning up the heat!" Riley said softly.

"Get your goat," added Sam.

"Then dive in," they said together. "Sharks don't take defeat."

Then dive in, then dive in, then dive in, then dive in, I said to myself. I went up the steps to the board. I stepped out onto the diving board.

"Get your goat," Sam said, just loud enough for me to hear.

"Then dive in," I said.

And I did.

Another glorious dive from Carmen Bernstein! I heard a sports announcer's voice in my head. It felt so good underwater.

I took my time coming back up. When I did, Riley, Sam, Brooklyn, and Rachel were all beaming at me. If they'd said anything, it would have totally ruined the moment. I tried to act all casual.

Sam pushed an inner-tube toward me.

"Time for the Dive-In movie!" he said.

We all got situated in our inner tubes. The lights dimmed just a little bit, and *Ferris Bueller's Day Off* started playing. It's an old classic from the 1980s and everybody has seen it about twelve times by the time they reach high school. Somehow that made it the perfect movie for a pool party. We didn't really have to pay attention because we basically had it memorized. It didn't matter that the sound was scrappy or that the picture was grainy on the wall. Nothing really mattered because we were all having fun.

Later that night, I was back home with Mom. After we watched *The Midnight Show* (which actually comes on at 11:35), I headed to my bedroom. I took a short detour by the bathroom to get a silver link bracelet I've had for a while but never worn.

In my bedroom, I pulled the star journal out of my workout bag. I got the charm out of my pocket and stuck it on the bracelet. It seemed like the perfect time to start wearing it.

"Come on, Murph. Time for bed," I called to my dog. He bounded up the stairs from the living room couch and flopped onto my bed. He was immediately asleep. I pushed him over a bit to make room for me.

I curled up with Murphy and my new journal. I fingered the shark charm on my bracelet. The charm felt good. The journal felt good, too. I'm such a blogger, but

I like the idea of writing on actual paper. I like the idea of making a book.

I still don't know where that weird message came from: the one with the processed cheese, goat, and dive. I'm sure now it wasn't from Riley, or Sam, or any of my friends for that matter. I'm not sure I care where it came from anymore.

All I know is that silly cheer somehow changed everything. It sounds corny, but from the day I got that message, I started seeing things I never noticed before. I have a nice stepsister and a cool stepbrother. I have the courage to try new things.

There was a bigger story that was going to go in this leather book. It was time for me to write that story. I was ready. It was ready.

I opened up the journal and wrote:

Carmen Dives In

4 ordinary girls
+ 4 mysterious messages
+ 4 crazy dares
= a whole lot of fun!

Nova Rocks!

Nova learns to follow her own dreams of becoming a rock star without breaking her mom's heart.

Carmen Dives In

When Carmen follows her mystery message, she discovers there may be more to her cheerleading stepsister than meets the eye.

Bright Lights for Bella

A mystery message helps Bella overcome her fear before she stars in the school play.

Rani and the Fashion Divas

Rani takes a chance and she finds something she never expected: a true friend.

Do a dare, earn a charm, change your life!

Ask for Star Sisterz books at your favorite bookstore!

For more information visit www.mirrorstonebooks.com

MORE ADVENTURES
FOR THE

FIGURE IN THE FROST

A cold snap hits Curston and a mysterious stranger holds the key to
the town's survival. But first he wants something…from Moyra. Will
Moyra sacrifice her secret to save the town?

DAGGER OF DOOM

When Kellach discovers a dagger of doom with his own name burned
in the blade, it seems certain someone wants him dead. But who?

THE HIDDEN DRAGON

The Knights must find the silver dragon who gave their order its name.
Can they make it to the dragon's lair alive?

**Ask for KNIGHTS OF THE SILVER DRAGON books
at your favorite bookstore!**

For ages eight to twelve

For more information visit <u>www.mirrorstonebooks.com</u>